Also by Susan Gabriel

Fiction

The Secret Sense of Wildflower
(a Kirkus Reviews' Best Book of 2012)

Lily's Song
(sequel to *The Secret Sense of Wildflower*)

Temple Secrets

Trueluck Summer

Grace, Grits & Ghosts: Southern Short Stories

Circle of the Ancestors

Quentin & the Cave Boy

Nonfiction

Fearless Writing for Women:
Extreme Encouragement & Writing Inspiration

Available at all booksellers
in print, ebook and audio formats.

Seeking Sara Summers

Susan Gabriel

Wild Lily Arts

Seeking Sara Summers

The author acknowledges permission to reprint the poem "Artichoke" from *The Undersides of Leaves,* by Joseph Hutchison, first published by Wayland Press in 1985.

Library of Congress Control Number: 2008932146

ISBN: 978-0-615-22207-3

Cover design by Thomjon Borges

Wild Lily Arts

For Anne

Artichoke

O heart weighed down by so many wings.

— *Joseph Hutchison*

Chapter One

Sara Stanton stopped at an intersection and stared at the red traffic light ahead of her. She wasn't the type to go off driving into the night. Not without a map and her destination circled in yellow highlighter. Her grin grew into a smile. She had managed to surprise herself. What if she just kept driving? The possibility intrigued her. She could be one of those people who went into the store to get a pack of cigarettes—in her case, a quart of Rocky Road—and never be seen or heard from again.

As her ten-year-old Volvo wagon vibrated its need for a tune-up, she adjusted the blue bandana that hid her new crop of short hair, the result of chemo. At home she wore bandanas but she wore a wig to school. Despite its similarity to her real hair she always felt that she was traveling in disguise. Doing some kind of undercover work investigating the criminally boring, of which she was a charter member.

Sara reached up and touched the vacant lot where her right breast used to be in a kind of pledge allegiance to the past. She had become a hybrid: part woman, part girl. Surgery had removed her right breast and the chemo had been tolerable. Besides the hair loss, it had produced only a mild, yet persistent, nausea over the weeks, accompanied by exhaustion. She was now in remission. But getting rid of the cancer in her body was the least of her worries.

She tapped the steering wheel with nails in need of another coat of polish and stared at the chip of a diamond in the engagement ring Grady had bought her twenty-five years before. He had offered to replace it on their 20th anniversary with something much bigger, much nicer. But she liked the simplicity of it and the time it represented. She could have worn Mimi's ring if she had wanted; her grandmother's 3-carat monstrosity. But she had saved it for her daughter, Jess. Or if Jess kept her adolescent promise to never succumb to marriage, she would give it to one of the boys for their wife-to-be.

The driver in the pick-up truck behind her beeped his horn. Sara threw the car into gear and accelerated through the small town she had lived in her entire life. She approached the street she and Grady had lived on for the last twenty years. She slowed, as she always did. She signaled to turn, as she always did. But then she didn't. She kept going. She drove out of town. She drove until the street lights ended and the road narrowed into a country road. Could a forty-four-year-old woman run away from home?

What are you doing? the voice began in her head. This was not a voice Sara liked very much. They rarely agreed on anything. *What about your responsibilities?* the voice continued. It was true. She had responsibilities. She had a husband, who right about now would be wondering about his ice cream that she had gone to the store to get. She also had six classes of high school English students, who relied on her to torment them with term papers and pop quizzes; a gaggle of drama students; numerous committees she served on, albeit unwillingly; various friends, none of whom she felt particularly close to; and the children, who were technically grown and out of the house. Not to mention, Doctor Evans, the marriage and family therapist Grady and Sara went to every Friday afternoon at 4:00, who relied on their weekly visits to help put his children through college.

Sara turned off her cell phone, anticipating Grady's call. Would he be more concerned about her or the fate of his Rocky Road? Their marriage had hit a rocky road itself two years before. It was a classic case of infidelity: long-term marriage, someone in his office, she offered, he acquiesced. The oldest story in the book. Sara was hurt at the time. But not nearly to the extent she would have expected. After that Grady had stopped working late. He spent more time at home.

And then she got cancer. By Grady's reaction, the "in sickness and health" part of their 25-year marriage had not included cancer. Sara had spent the last year apologizing for getting sick, apologizing for adding stress to his already stressful day.

In the last year Sara had taken stock of herself, as someone who takes stock of emergency supplies before a hurricane. Cancer was a shipwreck, she had decided, leaving survivors adrift at sea without drinking water, maps or oars. Every waking hour was spent in hope of rescue. Unfortunately, she had also discovered that she was ill-prepared for anything catastrophic—and was basically a coward. Not only about dying, but also about living. What did people do when they were absolutely sick of their lives?

Sara was driving too fast for the deserted country road but she didn't care. The head lights illuminated a dense layer of fog. Trees lined the road, creating a double layer of silvery darkness. Sara's giddiness took on a dark quality. She fantasized briefly about purposely losing control of the car and crashing into the trees. Death would probably be instantaneous. A sacrificial return to nature because she had failed at the one life given her.

Well, maybe not failed, she thought, *I just haven't shown up yet.*

Sara winced. When had she become so disappointed in herself?

Her death would go widely unnoticed. A small article in the local newspaper would relay the details of an ordinary life: the mother of three, teacher at the local high school, Girl Scout troop leader. . . *Blah, blah, blah*, went the voice in her head. Was that what a life came down to? A paragraph in the local paper?

What happened those days when she never gave life a thought? Her angst hidden beneath a flurry of endless activity. All three children had played soccer, resulting in countless hours spent on cold, hard school bleachers cheering them on. Not to mention a decade of school band concerts, music lessons and annual fund-raisers for their various activities that resulted in boxes of rotting citrus in their garage almost every Christmas. To this day, the sight of oranges and grapefruit made Sara slightly nauseous. Those years were a blur. A blur that now seemed blissfully void of self-examination.

Life had to be more than the day-to-day maintenance of a husband, kids and a community, she thought.

Sure there were moments of joy but most were quickly erased by the drudgery and hard work of life. Had there ever been any passion? Was her life ever really fun? Ever anything other than routine?

She accelerated again and rocked the steering wheel, swerving closer and closer to the trees on the edge of the road. She played at death the same way she played at life: afraid to commit. The tires suddenly grabbed at the shoulder. Dirt and gravel spewed from behind. Sara braked. She lost control of the car and desperately jerked it back onto the road. She missed one tree by inches. The second tree claimed the side mirror and scraped the side of the door. The car stopped. Adrenalin coursed through her body, accelerating her heartbeat and sending fireworks of hot tingles to her face.

Ice cream melted on the front seat. She took a deep breath; then another. A slight breeze dissipated the fog. The night became clearer.

You've got to be kidding me, Sara thought.

She laughed a brief, haunting laugh. The car had settled about a hundred feet away from a crossroads. Was the universe shoving the obvious in her face?

In the middle of the dark, deserted, New England countryside, she had suddenly found herself within the pages of a self-help book. She was at a crossroads in her life. Something had to change. She needed to go in a totally different direction. If she didn't, she feared for what would happen. The result felt as life-threatening as cancer.

Leaves clung to the wiper blades. It was fall in New England, the most beautiful time of the year, and she had hardly noticed. She chewed thoughtfully on a thumb nail. It would have been easier to crash into the trees. She didn't know how to start a new life. Especially if it involved giving up the old one.

Sara got out of the car and retrieved a flashlight from the trunk. The side mirror lay crushed at the base of a tree. She aimed the light toward the car. A deep silver scrape extended from where the side mirror used to be to the tail light. She wondered how

Grady would react. She had never even had a fender-bender in twenty-five years of marriage.

A set of headlights appeared in the distance. Sara got back in the car and revved the engine. She made a three-quarter turn driving slowly back toward town, tailpipe between her legs. Tears blurred the dark countryside.

So much for running away, she thought.

Like her youngest son, Sam, who at four years of age ran away from home and ended up in the tree house in the backyard, she had only gotten ten miles out of town.

The next morning students poured into her homeroom to beat the tardy bell. Sara's friend, Maggie, whose classroom was at the end of the hall, maneuvered her way across the room like a woman shopping the bargain basement intent on securing the best buys. Maggie's red hair, compliments of Clairol, set her apart from the crowd. She always wore green on some part of her body, as though every day was St. Patrick's Day and she might be pinched if found lacking.

"You look awful," she said.

"Gee, thanks," Sara said, her sarcasm giving her an odd satisfaction. "I didn't get much sleep," she added. Sara secured a loose strand of hair from her wig behind her ear; the same strand that always broke away from the rest. Was this intentional? she wondered. To make the wig seem more realistic?

"What happened to your car?" Maggie asked. "I saw it in the parking lot."

"I side-swiped a tree. Don't worry, the tree is fine."

"And Grady didn't kill you?"

"I haven't exactly told him yet." Sara raised her voice over the growing chaos in the room. She didn't mention the crossroads she had approached the night before. Or her disappointment in herself that she wasn't somewhere in Nova Scotia by now.

Sara turned an irritated gaze to her students, who could still be intimidated in their first year of high school. The volume of chatter decreased.

Maggie leaned against the edge of Sara's desk. "What's going on, Sara? Is the cancer back?"

"No, no," she said. "Nothing like that. I was just looking for a nail file to break out of this joint." When was it, she wondered, that she started hating her job?

The tardy bell rang. Maggie apologized. "I've got to go before my little angels start a Civil War." Maggie taught American History. She squeezed Sara's arm. "Don't worry, honey. You'll get through this."

Would she?

The door closed, leaving Sara as the only adult in a room full of twenty-four teenagers. *Never let them see your fear,* a mentor teacher had told Sara her first year of teaching. She squared her shoulders, retrieved her red pen from her satchel and opened the classroom roll book. For a few seconds she studied the captives in front of her. Was she ever like them?

A mixture of bravado and insecurity seeped out of their attitudes, speech, and their very pores, accentuated by piercings, tattoos, and fake hair colors to hide their middle-class roots. Following homeroom, several of these same captives would stay for her honors Freshman English class.

Sara raised her voice, "Settle down!" The roar of laughter and conversation subsided as if they instantly understood that today was not a day to challenge her. She enjoyed the power she had at first. But by the end of the first semester they had usually started to see through her.

Sara glanced out the windows that lined the entire wall. It was one of those schools built in the 50s that still had large, panel windows framed in dark wood, making the room freezing in winter and boiling in summer.

Ironically, as a teenager Sara had sat in this same classroom, a student of Mrs. McGregor's English literature class. She and her best friend Julia always sat together in the back of the room next to the windows. Day after day, they secretly made fun of Mrs. McGregor, a woman they considered older than Methuselah. When bored, they entertained themselves by keeping tally of Mrs. McGregor's wrinkles, making comic faces when they hit double digits. One day Sara's laughter had accidentally escaped into the room. A loud, honking footnote to Mrs. McGregor's lecture on *Beowulf*. Everyone turned to look at her as she ducked her chin to her chest and wished to disappear. Her face still turned hot just thinking about it all these years later.

Whatever happened to Julia? she wondered.

"Mrs. Stanton?"

Molly Decker slouched toward her, dressed entirely in black. Her black lipstick was in sharp contrast to the ivory makeup that covered a crop of pimples on her chin. *Would she find out some day that she wanted to run away from her life?*

"Yes?" Sara answered.

"Do we have drama after school today?"

"No, not today. I have to cancel," she said. Sara never cancelled anything. Not even in the throes of chemo. But the combination of really bad Shakespeare and her current angst seemed too much drama to bear today.

Insomnia robbed Sara of another night's sleep, as if a nightclub sign flashed the words *GET A LIFE* outside her window. She slipped from under the covers and stepped over Luke, their youngest son Sam's golden retriever—abandoned when Sam went away to college, never to be retrieved.

Moonlight came through the blinds and helped her find her way to her office downstairs, a home improvement project that had distracted them for months. An endless stack of papers to grade filled the extra chair in the room, a faded wingback beauty that Sara had found at a garage sale a decade before.

Bookshelves covered an entire wall where aging classics fought for space among the stacks of self-help books. She was always buying books that she never had time to read.

Sara searched the bottom desk drawer for a framed photograph of Julia and Sara as girls. After she found it she ran a finger along the glass to remove a layer dust. Sara stared into the past. At the time of the photo Julia's family was getting ready to move to England. Julia's eyes sparkled anticipating a new adventure, her arm around Sara's waist. Julia wore a pair of blue-jean overalls and red high-top sneakers. Julia had said once she wanted to be buried in that outfit, she loved it so much. And Sara had loved her.

Over the years Sara had wondered about Julia. But losing touch with people had become as habitual as losing touch with herself. She turned on the computer. Could she track Julia down on the internet? She had no idea if her childhood friend had married and used a different name. But what could it hurt? She typed *Julia David* into the search engine and waited for the response.

How easy it was to check on people these days, she thought.

She had typed in her own name on more than one occasion but there was nothing. Sara Stanton from Northampton, Mass didn't exist, as far as the world wide web could surmise.

Several references came up for Julia David. A few press releases about promotions, an article in an alumni magazine. Sara clicked on each reference. Evidently Julia had been an attorney in England for several years, specializing in high profile corporate cases. But the latest entries were of an artist in Florence. Was that Julia, too?

Sara smiled. She liked thinking of Julia in Italy. As a girl, Sara would have given anything to go to Italy. She had even written to the Italian Tourist Bureau and requested pamphlets, maps, anything Italian. Instead of teen posters of the heart throbs of the day, Sara had a map of Italy on her wall and a poster of the Duomo in Florence.

Sara continued her research, finally finding an email address for the Julia David in Florence. She started a new email and paused. What do you say to someone you haven't seen or talked to in almost thirty years?

Dear Julia,

Do you remember me? If you are the right Julia David, we used to be best friends nearly 30 years ago. We went to Beacon High School together.

If you have any desire to be in touch, please email back.

Your friend,
Sara (Summers) Stanton

It's worth a try, Sara thought, and sent the email.

She returned upstairs and turned on the light in the bathroom. She squinted into the mirror and tried not to notice how much she resembled her mother who had died of breast cancer when Sara was twelve.

Her mother's illness was kept hidden from Sara and her older brother until close to the end. Then one day they came home from school and their dad was waiting for them. Their mom was in the hospital. Doctors were running tests, he had said. Before Sara had time to see her again she had died. Would her mother have run away from home if she had had the chance?

Sara ran a finger along the slight crook in her nose that she had contemplated with disgust during her entire adolescence.

At least I inherited Mom's high cheekbones, she thought, *which served to redeem the nose.*

The hair growing in was dark blonde with streaks of gray. She had gone from a blond soccer mom hairstyle to a middle-aged punk rocker in a matter of months.

She pulled down her gown and studied the area where her right breast used to be. She had looked at it hundreds of times to get used to this new version of herself.

Mammary glands. That's all they are, she thought. *But why did everyone worship them? Two breasts were a commodity. One breast made a woman automatically less of a person.*

Sara turned off the light and walked down the dimmed hallway. At times, she felt like a character in a Charlotte Bronte novel, roaming the dark corridors at night. In the half-light she passed photographs of their children at different ages lining the walls. Jessica in her ballerina outfit—lessons lasted about as long as it took to take the photograph—John and Sam in soccer uniforms, Sam in his bigger brother's shadow, always looking up to him for approval. Not to mention every school photograph ever taken, complete with missing teeth and dated haircuts. Around the edges were a dozen photographs of Grady's family, most of them given to them by his mother, in contrast to only two of Sara's extended family. One of her father and Barb, his second wife, on their 10th wedding anniversary in a tacky teal frame with woodcut dolphins in the corners. And a black and white photograph of her mother posing in front of the diner their family owned in downtown Northampton, after it first opened. She wore a huge smile, held a cigarette in her left hand, and looked like a young Meryl Streep.

It had occurred to Sara to tell her dad and brother about her cancer but she didn't want to open old wounds. Ten years before her dad had sold the diner and had retired to Miami with Barb, a woman with as little interest in getting to know Sara as Sara had in getting to know her.

Barb was always giving them gifts of dolphin figurines. Dolphins jumping in mid-air while anchored to ceramic bases; dolphins in groups of three, jumping in tandem above waterless oceans; dolphins painted in the base of ashtrays given to a family where no one smoked. These figurines were stored in the back of the pantry and only brought out for their infrequent visits.

Five years older than Sara, her brother, Steve, owned a sea-food restaurant in Ogunquit, Maine, with Amy, his high school sweetheart, whom he had never officially married. He rarely got away from his restaurant and Sara rarely got over to Maine. Neither of them ever thought to call or write, so years would go by without any contact other than a card at Christmas. Despite bloodlines Sara and her brother were practically strangers. She doubted he would recognize her if they passed each other on the street. Especially now.

Sara stepped over Luke who always slept on the Oriental rug on her side of the bed. His tail thumped softly against the hardwood floor. She sat on the edge of the bed. In the darkness Sara placed a hand over where her breast used to be. Her next appointment was with a plastic surgeon to talk about reconstructive surgery.

But what I need reconstructing more than my breast is my life, she thought.

Who could help her with that? Most importantly, could you reconstruct a life that had never been there in the first place?

Chapter Two

Morning light filtered through the window creating tree-shaped shadows on the tile floor. House plants cluttered the seat of the bay window, some gangly and overgrown in their pots, and competed for the limited space with haphazard stacks of home improvement magazines.

Clutter gave birth to yet more clutter, spilling over from room to room, creating a constant need to organize the chaos—stacks of mail, papers, books, clothes—evidence of a consumer-driven culture gone awry. Beyond the bay window was Sara's attempt at a flower garden, an extension of the chaos inside.

Projects around their two-story, 1920s brick house had kept their marriage alive long beyond its natural shelf life. Grady and Sara had discovered that their marriage worked best when they were building something, whether it was a comfortable life, a future for their children, or an addition to their home. Intimate, detailed home improvement projects gave them a diversion from intimacy with one another.

"I want to organize the garage this weekend," Grady said. "But I'll need some shelves."

Sara poured them both a cup of coffee and joined him at the table in front of the bay window. "Why don't we go to Home Depot after we finish our coffee?" she said, surprised by her enthusiasm. For years she had wished for at least one unplanned Saturday where she could experience the contemplative solitude she had read about in books. Now the thought of having time to evaluate her life seemed cruel punishment.

Grady used the back of an envelope to make a list of the things he would need.

As long as he has the right tool for the job his life is complete, Sara thought.

He had no desire to question his manner of existence. No need for regrets. At that moment she envied his simplicity.

She looked at her engagement ring, remembering when they were first married. They had struggled financially for years and agonized about whether or not to buy their house. But they had been happy back then, hadn't they?

Sara and Grady arrived at the home improvement store early and roamed the aisles with the oversized shopping cart. Sara pushed the cart, rushing to keep up with Grady's pace as they moved quickly through this vast world of fixtures, tools and lumber.

"Grady, is there a reason we're going so fast?"

"I want to beat the crowds," he said.

"Crowds?" Sara asked. "The store is deserted."

Grady ignored her comment.

Sparrows chirped and flew among the rafters as if resigned to their captivity. Yet the large sliding doors opened frequently, giving them glimpses of freedom. Why didn't they make a break for it? Sara wondered. Was freedom that scary? She thought of her own need to escape. No, it wasn't that easy. Beyond those doors was something foreign and unknown. She felt compassion for the sparrows but little for herself.

His task completed, Grady approached his favorite cashier, a short, apple-shaped woman who looked like she existed on even less sleep than Sara did.

"There they are," she said to the younger woman next to her. "I was telling Jody you hadn't been in yet. But here you are, regular as clockwork. Every Saturday morning." The cashier in the next aisle smiled over at them. Her name, in bold letters, revealed the word "Trainee" underneath.

Grady's charm with other women always surprised her. Sara studied him for a moment, imagining what the cashier saw when she looked at her husband. Grady had aged well. His graying hair accented his blue/gray eyes and the five miles he ran religiously every morning kept him physically fit. She would never have guessed from knowing him as a gangly, awkward boy that he would mature into such a handsome man.

"How are you, Ginny?" Grady asked the cashier.

"They have me working a double shift," she said. "But I need the extra money." She scanned and bagged their purchases with the adept swiftness that came from making the same motions for years.

"Hi, Mrs. Stanton. How are you?" she asked, as if she had caught herself ignoring her.

"I'm fine," Sara said. "Sorry to hear about the double shift," she added. But her words had little impact.

"Well, I hope they're paying you double," Grady said.

Ginny's middle-aged face registered a glimmer of joy. "I wish," she said. She looked over at Sara and smiled wistfully, as if to cement her belief that all the good men were taken.

Sara took Grady's arm to solidify their image, a perfect commercial for marital bliss. It occurred to her that these were the times when they were closest, when they pretended to be someone else. No one suspected there might be something wrong with the picture they presented, not even Grady. No one questioned the fact that they were on their eighth home improvement project in two years, more home improvements per capita than anyone on their block. Even Ernie and David, the gay couple down the street, couldn't keep up with them. They came over periodically to see what Grady and Sara were working on and looked on in home-improvement admiration.

After their youngest child, Sam had left home—preceded by their daughter, Jessica, and oldest son, John—Grady and Sara had spent months adding on a sun porch to the back of the house. The sun porch addition had actually marked the darkest time of their marriage. Their nest now empty, they had been left without the material that had been holding them together for over two decades. But with the help of treated lumber and galvanized nails, they gave CPR to a relationship that had gone too long without oxygen. Meanwhile, Sara became better at convincing herself that nothing was wrong.

Then she got cancer. Cancer had forced her to take another look at her life. Like Ebenezer Scrooge, she had been given a glimpse of an empty future, where she lived a miserly rendition of what life could be. Yet it was the life the cashier at Home Depot dreamed about: a good job, a good husband, a house in a good neighborhood.

You're being unreasonable, the familiar voice began in her head.

Oh, shut up, Sara thought.

Why can't you be satisfied with what you have? the voice continued.
*Grady is a good man. Don't you see what you have? Don't you realize how
many other women would be perfectly content with a life like yours?*

Grady loaded his purchases into the back of his SUV while
Sara slid into the passenger side. She stared at the gas gauge on
the console as they drove home. How was it that Grady's gas tank
was always full? This required a diligence she couldn't imagine.
She was always running on empty. Lately her life had begun to
mirror this condition. Her so-called life had broken down and left
her stranded on the side of the road without the resources she
needed to carry on.

A crossroads, indeed, she thought.

Grady hummed along with a Bruce Springsteen song relegated
to the oldies station. Did he remember she was there? In her imagination she saw herself jumping out of the moving car. Crushed
under the axle of her expectations. Sara gripped the safety belt
across her chest to avoid the temptation.

You're getting dramatic in your old age, the voice clucked.

Sara sighed. *Perhaps a little drama is exactly what I need,* she
thought.

Grady turned down the radio. "Are you okay?"

*No Grady, I'm not okay. I'm having a conversation with a voice in my
head. I'm actually the farthest away from 'okay' I've ever been in my life. Why
can't you see that?*

"I'm fine," Sara said.

He turned the radio back up, and hummed the last refrain of
Born to Run.

They drove through the neighborhood that had changed very little during the twenty years they had lived here. It was a neighborhood adjacent to the one Sara had grown up in. She thought of Julia again, her girlhood friend. She hadn't thought of her in years and now twice in the last twenty-four hours. Wasn't Julia's parent's house three blocks over?

"Grady, can we go down Houser Street?"

He glanced at her, then shrugged and took the next block.

Julia had always collected strays—kittens, puppies, and birds—anything the least bit wounded. Sara was part of her flock, as was Grady.

Sara and Grady had grown up two streets west, in houses with the same floor plan, every other one transposed to make them appear different. Julia's house had been in an adjacent neighborhood marked by more trees and bigger houses, where no two looked alike.

The three of them had been best friends from fourth grade until their junior year in high school when Julia's family moved away. *The Three Musketeers* they had called themselves, as lame as it was. And then there were only two of them; Sara and Grady left behind like a two-legged stool. Why was she suddenly thinking so much about the past?

They married three years after Julia left. Sara had just turned twenty. It had been a small ceremony. Her father walked her down the aisle and sat next to his new wife, a woman very different from Sara's mother.

They drove in front of Julia's old house but Grady kept his eyes forward. Was he still mad at her for leaving? All these years later?

The small rose bushes Julia's mother had planted with Sara and Julia's help one hot August day were taller than Sara now. The oak tree they had climbed as children now had branches too tall to climb. And the red front door Julia had convinced her parents would look sophisticated, had been repainted by subsequent owners a smoky gray.

Julia always wore red—red shoes, red sweaters, red dresses—as if she owned a patent on the color. Red was not a color Sara considered wearing, even now. She preferred earth tones; colors that blended into the scenery. Red's vitality and passion was a moving target for the eyes of the world. Sara preferred safety over passion.

They turned onto their street. Ernie and David stood in their driveway unloading 2 x 4s from their white Land Rover. Grady beeped his horn and waved, then pulled in. "I'm just going to see what they're up to," he said to her. "Are you coming?"

"Not right now." Sara waved at the two middle-aged men who always looked like they had just stepped out of a Lands' End catalogue. They had been together as long as she and Grady.

Like boys in a locker room, the three men surveyed the length and width of the lumber. Grady laughed at something David said and put a leg up on the back of the Land Rover as if ready to stay for a while.

Sara's head ached a deep, nagging reminder of how disappointed she was with her life. She closed her eyes and rubbed her throbbing temples. Like a prospector panning for gold, she swirled the past, searching for any hints of an authentic life. Her thoughts returned to Julia. Memories of her old friend became a trail of bread crumbs that she might follow to find her way out of the forest.

Chapter Three

Grady stood over her in the flower garden, his body blocking the sun from Sara's face. "What's with you these days?" he asked. "You seem totally self-absorbed."

She rested her head on her knees. Until a year ago, when Sara discovered the lump, she had lived her life as though it had no expiration date. Those days were over. Sara hadn't told Grady about the twinge she had had the day before. Besides feeling physically odd, there was something else; an inner knowing that she hadn't put words to yet.

"I guess I am self-absorbed," she said. The sun warmed the crispness in the air. It was one of the last warm days of fall. The coming of winter always brought a slight melancholy for her. Winter seemed too perfect a metaphor for her marriage. She yearned to find a tiny bud of new life.

Sara had spent the morning pulling handfuls of weeds with a kind of reckless desperation, as if to rid herself of the regrets in her life.

Nearby, a small cluster of red flowers held onto the last days of bloom. The color red reminded her of Julia and of the email she had sent weeks before. She hadn't received a response.

An impatient look rested on Grady's face. "You think too much," he pronounced. He studied Sara as if she were a case file. Someone he had initially insured but lately had proven too risky a candidate.

"You're probably right," Sara said. "Oh, I almost forgot, your mother called while you were in the shower," Sara said. She wasn't in the mood for Grady's analysis.

He tucked his gray T-shirt into his jeans, the words *Stanton Insurance* faded on the front. His mother called him at least once a day to report on her miscellaneous aches and pains.

Maybe that's why he never seems to have room for mine, Sara thought.

Grady had taken over Stanton Insurance after his father retired. His office, located in downtown Northampton, was within ten minutes of their house. He often walked or rode his bicycle to work.

"Well I guess I'd better call her." Grady walked into the house. To the extent that Sara had an absent mother, Grady had a present one.

Later that night, Sara took Luke for a final walk of the day and came in the kitchen door. The door always stuck and required a hard push, using both hands and a knee to latch it. Sara and Grady had spent hundreds of hours on home improvements yet seemed to leave the little things unfixed.

Sara put Luke's leash on the hook in the pantry and refilled his water bowl. When she went into the bedroom Grady had showered and shaved. Sara sighed. Was she in the mood to make love?

She undressed and put on her nightgown. Then she sat on the bed and rubbed lotion onto her arms and legs, part of her nightly ritual. Grady ran a hand across her short hair—a gesture that reminded her of how he petted Luke—and climbed onto the bed behind her. He kissed Sara's neck. This was the moment she usually stopped him if she wasn't in the mood. But they hadn't made love since her last round of chemo, and she had missed being held.

Grady lowered her nightgown. He kissed her shoulders and rubbed them with the lotion sitting beside her on the bed. He never looked at where her breast used to be, nor would he touch the place where the cancer had lived. He focused on the perky, good breast; the breast that was left. She wanted him to acknowledge what had happened to her. Was this why Sara had hesitated about getting reconstructive surgery?

"You feel tense," Grady said. He deepened the pressure with his hands. "Do you want me to stop?" he asked, not stopping.

"No," she said. Grady could be tender when he wanted something. Sara closed her eyes, knowing the path his hands would travel and the sounds they both would make.

They rolled over in bed and briefly kissed; a fleeting flirtation between tongues. Sara always wished the kissing lasted longer. She longed for a deep, passionate exchange of fluids, instead of the brief mingling of their minty fresh toothpaste.

Grady entered her, his movements accelerating, as if it was his job to pump up their passion. Sara's mind wandered. She was suddenly reminded of Julia's father cranking the arm of their old-fashioned ice cream maker. Professor David had made peach ice cream every summer on the patio in their backyard. Julia and Sara would eat so much of it they would get ice cream headaches and collapse into their hammock together.

Julia's dad had taught European History at Smith College. He looked like a professor and always had a beard, even in the summer. Julia's mother had been her dad's teaching assistant and was twelve years younger. She was beautiful, as Julia was beautiful. Flawless skin highlighted by auburn hair that looked perpetually shiny, framing perfectly proportionate features.

"Why are you smiling?" Grady asked, his movement uninterrupted.

Should she tell him that she suddenly had an urge for peach ice cream? She reeled in her smile. "I was just enjoying you," Sara said.

Grady smiled. A drop of sweat rained down on where her right breast used to be.

Perhaps I can grow a new one from scratch, Sara thought.

Grady's breathing deepened as their ritual advanced. Sara imagined Julia in Florence. Was she married? Did she have children? Perhaps not. She had kept her maiden name.

"Grady, can you go deeper?" Sara said softly, surprising herself with this request.

Grady lifted up and decelerated, like a car shifting down a gear. "What?" he asked. His face was red. Sweat had gathered around his temples.

"Can you go deeper?" Sara whispered. She wanted deeper contact, deeper penetration. She wanted him to touch the part of her that was lonely and scared.

Grady groaned with enthusiasm and began again, putting more effort into his motions. It reminded her of the first time they had made love, a month after Julia had moved away. They had rocked the back of his red Chevy, as if the friction of their bodies might somehow be the magic to conjure Julia up again. Over the years they had graduated from cars, to dorm rooms, to their marital bed, which now creaked loudly with every thrust. Since the children had left there was a certain enjoyment to being louder than they used to be. Loudness, Sara supposed, that could be misinterpreted for passion.

Seconds later, the creaking bed stopped. Grady rolled to his side of the bed with a smile on his face and turned toward her.

"That was amazing," he said. "How was it for you?"

"Wonderful," she said, as she always did when he asked this question.

Grady kissed her lightly on the lips, and then rolled over to his side of the bed. Minutes later, he began to snore lightly. Hot tears filled Sara's eyes.

"I had hoped for better results," Doctor Morgan said. The head of the oncology department, he sat behind his large mahogany desk, more of a fortress than a piece of office furniture.

Absentmindedly, Sara stuck a finger into the pot of a plant on the edge of the desk to see if it needed water. She was always sticking her fingers into pots at home, afraid that she would find the evidence of her neglect. But in this instance she discovered that the plant wasn't real. Was the man in charge of her treatment someone who couldn't even keep a plant alive?

A framed photograph of a smiling boy in a blue baseball uniform sat next to the plant. She wondered briefly, given the status of the plant, if the picture had come with the frame.

Doctor Morgan removed his glasses to reveal brown eyes that matched the crescent moon of hair hugging the back of his head. "I recommend we repeat the series and up the dosage this time."

Sara smoothed her skirt and rested her hand on her right leg that had begun to shake. She took a deep breath. "What should I do in the meantime?" She sounded surprisingly calm at hearing she would not be retiring her bandanas anytime soon.

"What you're already doing," he said. "Eat right, exercise." He paused and walked from behind his desk to sit in the chair next to her. Sara automatically leaned back. It felt strange to have him so close. He patted her hand three times and then added a fourth, as if to fulfill the prescriptive measure. Had he learned this gesture in medical school during a crash course on bedside manner? Several awkward moments passed before he put on his glasses again and returned to his desk. She glanced at the fake plant which looked as robust as ever, a prop in the play that was her life.

Sara left his office and walked down a long white hallway and waited for the elevator. Once inside, she pushed *L* for *Lobby* and thought: *Life. Life Lost. Loser.* The cancer was back.

The doors opened in the expansive white lobby subsidized by cancer. It was filled with floor to ceiling windows, an assortment of larger fake plants, and a waiting area full of people flipping nervously through magazines.

Life is so tenuous, she thought, *and we fool ourselves into thinking it isn't.*

Her footsteps echoed in the parking garage, strangely deserted in the middle of the day. Sara called the school to tell them she wouldn't be back that afternoon and went home to an empty house, except for Luke, who was ecstatic to see her.

Sara grabbed his leash in the pantry and hooked him up for a walk. Walking helped her process things. It helped her think. Luke led the way around a large block in their neighborhood lined with older homes. He sniffed and revisited his habitual places, a favorite bush, the elm tree at the corner, and a concrete lion on a driveway at the end of the road.

Her appointment with Doctor Morgan played over in her mind. He had not said the words but the implication was there: to get her affairs in order. But what affairs? Except for her grandmother's ring, she didn't really own anything apart from Grady. He would take care of everything. If anything, they were overinsured, over-prepared for external disasters. It seemed the things Sara needed to get in order were internal things. But how do you make peace and assign meaning to a life that was spent merely sleepwalking?

You're being too hard on yourself, the voice said.

Well that's a switch, Sara thought. *If the critical voice in my head is defending me, I must really be in trouble.*

Back at the house, Iris Whitworth, an elderly neighbor, watched Sara from her dining room window. The old woman seldom bothered to hide her interest. Sara waved and the curtain closed.

"What will she do if she doesn't have me around to watch?" Sara said to Luke. She pulled her jacket closer. The weather was changing. Clouds covered the sun.

Sara went inside and filled a tall glass with tap water and drank it completely, hoping its basic elements would ground her. Out the kitchen window, snow with large, moisture-laden flakes filled the sky. Winter had arrived.

Minutes later the kitchen door slammed. Sara jumped as Grady walked into the kitchen.

"Didn't mean to scare you," he said.

"I was just deep in thought." Sara could count on Grady not to pursue what she had been thinking.

He placed his canvas briefcase on a kitchen chair and removed the bands from the legs of his pants that he wore when he rode his bicycle home. Flakes of snow melted at his feet. He sifted through the stack of mail on the table and asked about her day, not even looking up.

"It was uneventful, really." She lied. She would not tell Grady what the doctor had said, at least not yet.

For the first time Sara noticed that she and Grady were dressed alike. He wore a white shirt with his khaki pants. She wore a white sweater with her khaki skirt. Their pale faces emerged from an unintentional forest of yuppie camouflage.

Grady loosened his green tie dotted with small red peppers, a Christmas gift from their daughter, Jessica. Grady often received ties as gifts. His growing collection had taken over their closet. Despite the vertical strip of color dividing his chest, he always looked the same.

Birds visited the feeder outside the kitchen window. Sara made dinner, numb to her surroundings. During their usual silence at the dinner table Sara's finite life felt unending. News reports blared on the small television that sat on a nearby counter. Voices on the television took the place of their own. Far away disasters distracted them from the quiet one right there in the room.

She thought of the sparrows in the rafters of the home improvement store and pushed the winter squash from one edge of her plate to the other. "You know, I've never liked squash," she said, to break the silence.

Grady looked up. He chewed thoughtfully and then swallowed. "Then why do you fix it so often?" he asked.

"I'm not sure," she said. "I guess because you like it."

"I don't like it either," he said.

They grinned at each other, as if they had caught themselves in the lie they had been living.

After dinner, Sara retreated to her office to grade term papers. With felt-tip pen in hand, she began with the paper on top; Molly Decker's dark critique on the book *Little Women*, where she insisted that hidden within the pages of the classic was Jo March's Goth agenda.

Was I ever this intense? Sara thought. Perhaps her life would have gone better if she had been.

Two hours later, she had only finished eight of the twenty-four she had to grade. She rubbed her eyes and turned on the computer. She checked her email. A new message from a *J. David* appeared in her Inbox.

Sara gasped. "Julia?" she asked, as if the email might answer her.

Dear Sara,

What a wonderful surprise! Of course I remember you!! How could I forget? We were practically joined at the hip when we were growing up.
HOW ARE YOU??

Sorry I haven't answered sooner. I have an art show coming up and I've just been swamped with getting pieces ready. But it is so great hearing from you after all these years.

What have you been up to?

Did you do all that traveling you wanted to do when you were a girl?
TELL ME EVERYTHING!

On a different note, I sent you something in the mail last week. You
should get it soon if you haven't received it already.

Your friend,
Julia

P.S. So can I assume from the Stanton on the email that you married
our old friend, Grady?

Sara smiled and searched her memory for details about Julia:
the way she laughed, the way she wore her hair. She wondered if
they would still be friends if she had never moved away. As it
was, their friendship had ended quietly, like two boats drifting
away from a dock, each carried by a different current. After she
left, Sara had ignored Julia's efforts to contact her. She had secretly
hated her for moving away the summer before their senior year,
even though it was through no fault of her own. Her father had
accepted a prestigious teaching position in England. At the time
Sara hadn't been the least bit happy for her. She had been too
devastated at being left behind.

Sara hit reply.

Dear Julia,

It's so nice to hear from you! I'd convinced myself my email had never
arrived. Or that you'd long ago trashed it because you didn't remember me.

Grady cleared his throat as he stood at the door watching her.

Sara jumped for the second time that day. "I didn't hear you there," she said. "Did you finish?"

"Everything I wanted to get done tonight," he said.

Grady had been in his workshop building new kitchen cabinets. He pulled off his T-shirt and wiped the sweat from under his arms. The dark hair in the middle of his chest was slightly graying. There were flecks of sawdust on his arms, earthy glitter held in place by the sweat. Sara's memory flashed on a younger Grady. Skinny, with a chest devoid of hair, and prominent ribs—even though he had eaten as much as her and Julia combined—and an even more prominent Adam's apple.

"Did you make an appointment to get the car fixed?" Grady asked.

"Not yet," she said. It had been weeks since her little run-in with the tree. Grady had been very calm about it when she had finally told him, his only comment being about how good their insurance was.

"Is there some reason you don't want to get it fixed?" he asked.

"Of course not," Sara said. But was there? Perhaps it was proof that she had almost gotten away. "I'll get it done next week. Dented cars just aren't high on my priority list right now." Her number one priority was simply getting through the day.

"Are you coming to bed?" he asked.

"As soon as I finish."

"Tons of papers to grade tonight?"

"The usual." What wasn't usual was for Grady to be this in-quisitive. If she didn't know better she would think that some part of him had intuited that Julia had been in touch.

"Well, goodnight then," he said.

"Goodnight," she answered. Sara listened for his footsteps ascending the carpeted stairs before continuing the email.

... I did marry Grady. After you left we stayed friends and we both ended up going to U Mass. We have three children. They're all grown up and have left home—two boys and a girl. Sam's the youngest, he's 22. Jessica's 23 and John is 24. Jess and Sam work in New York City at the same investment firm and John is in law school in Boston. They're great kids. I think you would like them. It's still hard for me to believe I had any part in creating such beautiful, smart human beings. It's also hard to believe that part of my life is over now. The house is very quiet these days.

Sara debated what else to say. There had been a time when Sara could tell Julia anything. Should she tell her about the cancer? Or about how her life just didn't make sense anymore?

She wrote a paragraph about her illness and then quickly deleted it. It was too soon to share something so intimate. She began a new paragraph.

... Julia, I love thinking about you being in Florence. Remember my obsession with Italy years ago?

It is wonderful to hear from you again. I look forward to getting whatever you sent. Meanwhile, tell me anything and everything about Italy!

Your friend,
Sara

Sara sent the email and then turned off the computer and the light. As she climbed the stairs an unexpected lightness filled her. She smiled again. Julia had remembered her.

Sara grabbed Luke's leash, deciding to give him a quick walk instead of just letting him out in the backyard. It was dark. An inch of snow covered everything. Luke peed on the dogwood close to the porch, a standard practice, while Sara retrieved a bundle of mail in the brass mailbox mounted next to the front door. She sorted through a stack of junk mail. The light bulb on the porch had burned out weeks before but neither Sara nor Grady could seem to remember to replace it. The nearby streetlight helped illuminate the sorting.

Hiding behind a pizza coupon was a blue envelope. Sara ran a finger along the letter's parameters. Its blue elegance stood out in glaring contrast to the junk mail and bills in her hand. She admired the precise handwriting and lovely color of the envelope before realizing that the letter had an Italian postmark.

This must be what Julia was talking about, Sara thought.

Inside the envelope was an invitation to an art opening along with a handwritten note.

Dear Sara,

I know it's a long shot but I thought I'd send you an invitation to my art opening in April.

It was so nice to hear from you recently. I have been thinking of you and remembering the things we used to do as girls. We had a lot of fun, didn't we?

I hadn't given my past much thought until now. I guess I'm becoming more reflective in my old age. (Ha! Please don't tell me we're getting old!)

    Ciao,

    Julia

Luke tugged at the leash and Sara crammed everything back into the small brass mailbox except Julia's letter. She clutched the envelope to her heart. Her energy increased with each step down the walkway. Sara had to resist the urge to skip. What if she went to Italy?

Don't be ridiculous, the voice in her head chimed in.

But the mere possibility caused Sara's joy to bubble into a laugh. She walked several blocks in the dark moving in and out of the glare of streetlights, a clear destination in mind. She stopped in front of Julia's old house while Luke sniffed the rose bushes and christened them.

Sara remembered an earlier time when she and Julia had caught lightning bugs in the front yard. One summer they put them in jars thinking they would light up Julia's bedroom. Instead, they had all died by morning. Sara still felt bad about that and had not let her children participate in the practice.

Sara stared into her past. She and Julia had sat on those very steps swearing on a blood oath—*well, not really a blood oath,* Sara thought, *I had been too chicken for that*—but they had squeezed the promise into each other's clasped hands that they would move away from their little town some day and travel the world having adventures.

I didn't keep my promise, Sara thought.

But maybe it wasn't too late. She jogged back to the house with more energy than she had had in months, and greeted Grady in the kitchen with an embrace.

Chapter Four

Grady was in the kitchen having his habitual nightly bowl of Rocky Road. This meant it was eight o'clock.

"You're in an awfully good mood," Grady said. "Did we win the lottery?"

Sara ignored his sarcasm. "I just heard from an old friend of ours, and she's invited me to come to an art opening in Italy." The boldness in her voice surprised her.

"Italy?" He laughed a short laugh and looked up as though waiting for a punch line.

"Actually, Florence," Sara said.

Grady returned the ice cream container to the freezer and leaned against the counter, his spoon clicking against the side of the bowl with his first bite.

"What old friend do we have in Italy?"

"Julia."

Her name bounced lightheartedly across the room and landed like a stone at Grady's feet. His brow furrowed. "How is Julia?" He put down his bowl of ice cream as if it had suddenly soured.

"She's doing very well." Sara felt protective of her old friend and didn't go into the details of their correspondence.

"So Julia's in Italy," Grady said thoughtfully. "I always wondered where she ended up."

"Yes, Julia's in Italy, and I've decided to go and visit her," Sara said, her fledgling confidence bolstering her boldness.

Grady set his jaw and jiggled the keys in his pocket, a melodious sign of his impatience. "Are you serious?" he said. "How in the world would we ever afford a trip to Italy? Not to mention how busy things are at work right now."

"Actually, the invitation was to me." Sara's voice lost some of its energy.

For a brief second his face flushed, as if he should have been the one to receive the invitation instead of her. "Do you have money I don't know about?" he asked coldly.

What was left of Sara's enthusiasm drained away, like water out of a bathtub. Her shoulders dropped. The trip was totally impractical; and in their household practicality trumped dreams.

Sara grasped the invitation in her jacket pocket and a flutter of energy returned. Sara stood straighter, challenging herself to look him in the eye. "You know, Grady, sometimes a person just has to do something totally illogical."

"Well, more power to you if you can figure out the finances. All our credit cards are totally maxed out." He sat down at the table and rifled through the mail, dropping the subject of Julia like a piece of dirty laundry on the floor. He was making the trip about money, yet somehow Sara knew it wasn't about money at all.

"Why do you hate Julia so much?" she asked.

"I don't hate Julia." His voice momentarily softened. "It's just a ridiculous idea. Why would she be in touch after all these years, anyway? What does she want?"

"Nothing," she said. Sara never thought she would have to defend Julia to Grady. "For your information, I was the one who got in touch with her a few weeks ago."

"So now she finally has time for you?"

"What is this really about?" Sara asked. "Are your feelings hurt? Are you upset that Julia asked me to come instead of you?"

"Julia never cared about me," he said.

His anger felt old. He was a jilted teenage boy again. "Is that really what you believe?" Sara asked.

He glared at her, his Adam's apple erect. "You two always were against me," he said.

"Where's that coming from?" Sara asked. "Julia loved you like a brother. We both did."

"Is that what I am to you, Sara, a brother? A brother who doesn't know what's best for you?"

"What's best for me?" Sara wanted to slap him. "Since when do you get to say what's best for me?"

"Since forever," he said. "You wouldn't know how to make a decision if your life depended on it."

Sara grabbed a clean pan sitting on the stove and hurled it in his direction. It missed him by about six inches and bounced at his feet. The sound echoed the sharpness of her emotion.

"What's gotten into you?" He stepped back.

"Maybe a little backbone." Sara slammed the cabinet door that had never closed properly and one of her mother's china tea cups fell to the floor and shattered.

"That was intelligent," he fumed. "You hear from Julia and you suddenly become an idiot."

"And you become a jerk!" Sara countered.

Sara had never, in twenty-five years of marriage, called Grady a jerk. He grinned, as if her reaction had secured the final piece of evidence needed to pronounce her thoroughly unreasonable.

But Sara had gone too far to turn back. The Pandora's Box of their marriage had flung open, their denied issues escaping into the room. "I'm so sick and tired of you limiting me. And of *me* limiting me. Something has to change, Grady. I just can't live like this anymore." Her bottom lip quivered a signal that tears were next.

"Live like what?" His voice rose to match hers.

"Just pretending that everything is all right. Pretending I never had cancer. Pretending we have this great marriage . . ."

Grady's jaw released, as if Sara had delivered an unexpected left hook and the knock-out blow that could cost him the match. The sharp edge of his silence followed. The blue and white tiles on the kitchen floor held Grady's gaze. Tiles they had put down in the weeks after her cancer diagnosis. The remnants of Sara's boldness quickly dissolved.

Their marriage lay on the floor like a dead body they were both afraid to touch. What was she thinking? She couldn't go to Italy. The trip no longer made sense. A train had derailed in their kitchen. Sara had to stay and attend the wounded. Didn't she?

"Grady, I'm sorry if I hurt you." Sara touched his shoulder. He turned away, but not before shooting her an angry look. She had broken an unspoken rule in their marriage. She had told the truth.

"Julia always did know how to shake things up," he said.

"This isn't about Julia," Sara said softly. "It's about us."

Her words were met with silence. Something had happened that she and Grady hadn't planned. Something that they didn't know how to recover from in ten minutes of Psych 101 chitchat and simple reassurances. It felt like one of those necessary, but regrettable, moments when you know you've said too much. And when you know you haven't protected the other person from some nastiness in yourself.

"Maybe we should deal with this in Doctor Evan's office," Sara said.

"I agreed to go to counseling," Grady said, "but I don't think it's doing any good."

"Then what are we supposed to do?"

The blue wall clock over the kitchen sink ticked away the seconds in the background. "Maybe you should go to counseling," he said.

"Me?"

He crossed his arms; a judge about to pronounce a verdict in a case. "Ever since you got sick you've been different, Sara."

"You mean ever since I got cancer? Are you afraid to say the word?"

"You're just not satisfied with things anymore," he said.

"I'm surprised you noticed." Sara regretted the words as soon as she said them. She bit her bottom lip and relaxed her hands that had worked their way into fists.

"Grady, I'm sorry," she said again.

He turned and walked away.

Two days after their fight the lifeless body of their marriage still lay in the kitchen where they each dealt with it in their own ways. Sara, with her morbid fascination with its decomposition. Grady, choosing to step over the corpse and pretend it didn't exist.

Silence became their drug of choice, until the dead quiet between them finally wore itself out and they began to speak again
of ordinary things. They returned to a life of polite, respectful in-
teraction. It wasn't a horrible life, Sara decided. Not heaven or
hell, but more like a marital purgatory.

The telephone rang that night during dinner. They glanced at
each other. Neither of them made a move to pick up the extension
in the kitchen. After several rings, Grady finally went to answer it.

"Stanton residence," he said formally.

His face turned ashen. Sara suddenly worried that something
had happened to one of their children. She rose from the table
anticipating car crashes, broken hearts and broken bones.

"What a surprise," Grady said finally. His voice wavered, but
then his formality returned. "Sara said just the other day that she'd
heard from you."

Sara froze momentarily and then stepped closer.

"I'm fine. No complaints." Grady laughed and ran a hand
through his hair like he used to when he was younger. He suddenly
seemed boyish.

There could only be one person who could make Grady react this way,
Sara thought.

"Yes, Sara's right here. Hold on, please."

Grady handed her the telephone. For several seconds Sara
simply looked at it. In general, she didn't like surprises. Not even
good ones. Grady nudged her to speak. "Julia?" she asked weakly.

"Yes, Sara, it's me!" Julia's exuberance vibrated through the
phone line.

Three decades of emotions rushed forward. They were girls
again, playing in Julia's backyard. Julia had yelled "Freeze!" and at

her command Sara became a statue, holding her features in an unblinking daze. To have her call was as if Julia had suddenly yelled, "Unfreeze!" and Sara's life had resumed again after thirty years.

"Sara, are you there?" Julia asked.

Her voice sounded familiar and unfamiliar at the same time. "Yes, yes, I'm sorry," Sara said. "It's just so strange to hear your voice again. It's like coming face to face with a ghost. Or should I say, ear to ear." Sara laughed, and then grimaced at her lame joke.

"I guarantee I'm not a ghost," Julia said. "I'm sitting right here in the flesh."

"Are you in New England?"

"No, Italy." Julia paused, as if waiting for Sara's fledgling exuberance to catch up to hers. "Well, Grady sounds the same."

"I think you surprised him," Sara said.

"I'm sure I did." Julia's tone implied more than Sara had the wherewithal to pursue. Julia asked how she and been and Sara responded in ways that she might have given a stranger on the street. It occurred to her that she was saying all the wrong things. But at that moment Sara felt incapable of anything more. Trapped in a time warp, she was both forty-four and sixteen.

"Are you okay?" Julia said, her voice softer.

Sara reassured Julia she was fine. "I just never expected you to call."

"They have phones in Italy, you know." Julia's voice was playful, dynamic.

Grady leaned in closer; his breath touched her shoulder. Sara resisted the urge to swat him away. They were a triangle again, Julia at its apex.

"It's so nice of you to call," Sara said.

Why did she sound like she was talking to someone trying to get her to change her long distance service? This was Julia, the best friend she hadn't seen or spoken to in nearly thirty years.

"I think I caught you at a bad time," Julia said, her exuberance fading. "I just wanted to make sure you got my invitation."

"I did," Sara said. "I'm afraid I can't make it. But I'm sure it will be lovely."

Seconds passed where Sara promptly forgot everything she wanted to say. It was the most disastrous phone call of her life. The shock of Julia's call had caused a massive exodus of crucial brain cells. It didn't help that Grady had suddenly become clingy.

Sara hadn't realized until that moment how much she had missed Julia. So much so she could feel it in her chest, throbbing beneath the scar that had turned a light, glossy pink over the months. But the emotion refused to translate into words. Sara had morphed into the most boring person alive, attempting a conversation with the most vibrant.

"Well, it's late," Julia said finally.

They said their goodbyes, promising to keep in touch. After Sara hung up the receiver, Grady relaxed, as if a soldier going from attention to at-ease and Sara went rigid.

"I can't believe she telephoned," Grady said. "What's it been, like thirty years?"

"Almost." Sara couldn't believe he wanted to talk about it.

"It had to be midnight in Italy when she called," he said. Grady found it difficult to stay up past ten.

"Julia always liked staying up late. Even on school nights." It seemed odd that Sara would remember details about Julia, given there were crater-sized gaps in her own childhood memories.

"I never knew that about her," Grady said thoughtfully.

It was the closest Sara had ever seen Grady to being reflective. They hadn't spoken of Julia since her invitation had arrived. And before that it had been decades since her name had come up.

"We probably won't hear from her again for another thirty years," Grady said.

Sara still had the receiver in her hand. Grady walked over and kissed the top of Sara's head, as if their fight from two days before was suddenly forgiven. His lips lingered longer than she expected. "Your hair smells nice," he said softly.

This gesture felt too intimate for them. Had Julia's call made him nostalgic for their old semblance of togetherness?

"I'm going to bed," he said, the spell broken.

How could I have been such a total idiot over the phone? she thought.

She made herself a cup of herbal tea and thought of all the things she should have said if she hadn't totally lost her mind during the call.

Ironically, earlier that day Sara had decided not to email Julia again. But then the universe had mysteriously wrapped around itself. Instead of saying goodbye to Julia, she was actually saying hello.

When Sara went into the bedroom, Grady was already sleeping, his book resting on the chest. She removed his reading glasses from his nose and laid them with his book on the nightstand. It was ten o'clock exactly. He would rise refreshed at 6:00 A.M., after a full eight hours sleep, ready for a morning run. She smiled at the absurdity of sleep after the phone call from Julia. But she went through the motions anyway, just in case her mind was exhausted enough to allow her to rest.

Moments later Sara had a vague sense of longing. Grady lay a few inches away, yet she missed him. More exactly, she missed the relationship they could have had if they had been different people.

Before turning out the light, she went to the closet and pulled out the jewelry box that had been her grandmother's. She took out Mimi's ring. It had been an unexpected inheritance a decade before. At the time, Sara had had it appraised and found out that it was worth as much as a new car. She had never told Grady this. It had felt good to have something of her own.

Sara observed the man sleeping next to her: the graying hair at his temples, the creases on his forehead that had grown deeper over the years, the slight smile on his face when he slept. He was happiest when he was unconscious.

She closed the lid of the jewelry box and returned it to the shelf behind all of Grady's ties. Was she really considering selling the ring and going to Italy for Julia's art show?

Chapter Five

Inside the airport, Sara adjusted the travel bag on her shoulder. The strap slid off with nagging frequency. "I can't believe I'm actually doing this," she said to her daughter, Jess.

"You deserve it, Mom. Except I don't see why we had to get here four hours early."

"I didn't want to miss my flight," Sara said.

"That would be pretty impossible." Jess smiled, as if acknowledging another of her mother's ridiculous traits she had put up with her entire life. Spontaneous risk-taking was Jessica's mode of operation. Sara's risks took thirty years to pull off.

"It's so sweet of you to come see me off, honey."

"It's no big deal. I work in the city. Besides, I don't want that guilt you're famous for to stop you from going."

"I hope you don't hate me for selling Mimi's ring," she said.

"Mom, for the thousandth time, it's okay. I would have never worn that gaudy thing anyway."

Jess was fit and muscular from all her workouts at the gym and exercised as religiously as her father. She also reminded Sara of her mother sometimes if she turned her head a certain way.

Sara pushed a strand of her daughter's blonde, shoulder-length hair behind her ear the way she had when she was a girl. During Jess' stormy adolescence, Sara wouldn't have attempted this.

"So your flight goes from New York to Milan?" Jess asked.

"Yes, then from Milan I'll take the train to Florence. I can't even believe I'm saying this, Jess. Am I really going to Italy?"

"Relax, Mom. People do it all the time."

"I don't think I ever told you that when I was a girl I dreamed about going to Italy. I was practically obsessed about it."

"Really?" Jess said. "You never told me anything about when you were a girl."

"Sometimes I forget I actually was one," Sara said.

Jessica popped her gum. "You must get tired of being so serious all the time."

Sara laughed and hugged her. "Yes, actually I do."

They stood in silence, watching the bustle around them. The scene reminded Sara of when Jess first went away to college. She and Grady had delivered her to the steps of the freshman dorm, and then they were somehow supposed to drive away.

Now, it seemed, their roles had reversed. Sara was the one at the crossroads and dropped off on the doorstep of a new adventure. She smiled at the melodramatic ease with which she analyzed life these days. Cancer had given her permission to indulge herself.

"I'd better check in," Sara said. A sensation registered in her chest, like a bird knocking its wings against the bars of its cage. She took a deep breath. "Why don't you give your dad a call later and check on him."

"Is he still pissed at you?"

"I'm pretty sure that's what his silence means."

"He'll get over it," Jess said. "He's just used to getting his way."

Grady had left the house early, stepping around her luggage in the hallway, without saying goodbye. No wishes of safe flights, or good trips.

The week before, Sara had considered inviting him to come along. Induced by guilt rather than genuine desire, this invitation would have undoubtedly created a mooring for the rough seas she wasn't so sure their marriage could weather. But in the end she had decided that this trip had nothing to do with Grady. She had deemed it her farewell tour. She would use whatever time she had left to erase the regrets in her life.

She was going to Italy. A place she had dreamed about going since she was a girl. She would surprise the best friend she had ever had in her life by showing up at her art show opening. If Grady's ego couldn't take that, then she didn't care.

"I may need your help if I get back and all my things are on the lawn," Sara continued.

"Like Daddy would ever let the neighbors know there was a problem. Most of them are his customers." Jess rolled her eyes, a gesture that Sara had hated when she was an adolescent, but now seemed endearing again. "Is your friend picking you up at the airport?"

"She doesn't even know I'm coming."

"She doesn't know you're coming? Mom, this whole thing is just so out of character for you," she said.

"Thanks," Sara said. She liked doing things out of character because it meant she had character to begin with. But her smile hid the terror she felt.

"Mom, is there something you're not telling me? You're okay aren't you? I mean with the whole C thing."

Sara hadn't told anyone about her last trip to Doctor Morgan or that as soon as she returned she would be going through another round of chemo, a more aggressive round.

"No, honey. I'm fine. The whole C thing is taken care of." Why this sudden inability to be truthful? Sara wondered. Was she trying to protect them or protect herself?

Jess looked relieved and popped her gum again. "Well, I'd better get back to work," she said.

"Thanks again for seeing me off," Sara said. They embraced and for the next few seconds Sara soaked in their reconnection.

"Ciao!" Jessie smiled as she walked away.

"Ciao!" Sara laughed in response. "I love you, honey!" she called after her.

Sara walked toward the airline check-in. Her stomach tensed. Second thoughts bombarded her. She could still catch Jess if she turned back now. Julia would never know she had backed out of the trip. She didn't expect her anyway. But Sara had sold Mimi's ring. She had taken a sabbatical from work. She had managed to surprise everyone she knew, including herself. No turning back, she told herself. If you don't do this now, you'll never do it. She willed herself forward.

Sara passed through security and reached the boarding area. Two hours later her flight was called. Sara found her seat next to a large man wearing earphones. He had the demeanor of a businessman who had taken countless flights, eaten his weight in fast food, with little time to exercise. He smelled heavily of cigarettes and a box of nicotine gum bulged in his shirt pocket. His bulky arm on the armrest forced Sara to lean into the window.

It was an evening flight; pillows were in every seat. The possibility of Sara sleeping through the night and waking up in Italy seemed remote, at best, considering the level of excitement—laced with fear—coursing through her body.

"Can I get you anything?" the flight attendant asked. Had she noticed how nervous Sara was? She looked Italian, perhaps in her early 30s, her hair and eyes dark, her features striking.

Perhaps a tranquilizer, Sara wanted to say.

Her right knee began to shake and she placed her hand there to calm it.

As they sat on the runway the captain's voice came over the loudspeaker to welcome them aboard. Perhaps they had an Italian crew taking them to Milan. The pilot's English, while impressive, revealed his primary language underneath. Sara liked the idea that their crew was on their way home to wives and children and loved ones. In an odd way, it was as though she was on her way home, too. Sara didn't even know Julia anymore, but at the same time she had missed her.

Flight attendants served drinks and a meal, rolling carts in steady increments up and down the aisles. Did they ever get bored with their jobs?

The perpetual cheerfulness required would drive me insane, Sara thought.

A family sat in the center seats across the aisle. A husband and wife, she assumed, and a girl of about six or seven between them. The girl thumbed through the pages of a book, her head resting against her mother's shoulder. Scenes of mothers and daughters often captivated Sara's imagination. Had she ever rested her head against her mother's shoulder like that? She couldn't remember.

As they flew across the Atlantic, the businessman beside Sara ordered several vodka tonics and watched the in-flight movie. The lights were dimmed. From her window seat Sara stared out into the dark night, imagining the ocean below.

Periodically, the moon revealed patches of smooth clouds with stars behind them.

Star light, star bright, Sara thought.

Hadn't she and Julia recited that as girls? She closed her eyes and rested into her memory.

"Look at those stars," Julia said. "The sky is full of them."

"They're amazing," Sara whispered. She had been spending a lot of time at Julia's since her mom had been sick. Her 12th birthday had been the day before and the charm bracelet Julia had given her dangled loosely around her wrist.

Julia and Sara lay on their backs in the soft grass of summertime, studying the universe from Julia's backyard. A square patch of light reflected from the kitchen window. The only other light came from the moon.

"There are probably two girls in Paris looking at the stars just like us," Julia said.

Sara sighed, the image pleasing her. Julia's view of the world was always bigger than hers.

"Hey, let's make a wish," Julia said.

Julia took Sara's hand, their fingers interlocking to make the magic more powerful. They said in unison, "Star light, star bright. First star I see tonight. I wish I may, I wish I might, have the wish I wish tonight."

They made their wishes in silence, their hands squeezed tightly, as if this were required to thrust their intentions into the universe. With a final squeeze,

Julia released Sara's hand. Then she rolled over and looked at Sara, resting an arm under her head. "What did you wish for?" she asked.

"You're not supposed to tell, or it won't come true," Sara said. She missed the warmth of Julia's hand.

"Come on, Sara, tell me," she insisted. "A wish among friends is sacred. Nothing can keep it from coming true."

"I don't want to jinx it."

"Tell me," she said again.

Sara hesitated. "I wished . . . that my mother wasn't sick anymore."

Julia reached over and squeezed Sara's hand again. Then leaned on one elbow and caressed her hair. "It'll be all right, Sweetie."

Sara's tears blurred the stars. She didn't know what she'd do without Julia. She was more like family than her own family was these days. She wiped away the tears. "What did you wish for?" Sara asked.

"I'm not telling," Julia said. "It may not come true." Her giggle escaped into the darkness.

"You bum!" Sara rolled over and tickled Julia who squealed her protest. "What was it?" Sara asked again.

"I'll never tell," Julia giggled. Their laughter dissolved into the summer breeze. Sara was captivated. Not only by the vast, starry night, but by the vastness of their friendship.

Sara opened her eyes. Her smile reflected in the window and for a fleeting moment she saw the girl she used to be. The jet engines hummed steadily. Sara tugged at her hair, willing it to grow. This length looked almost fashionable. At least she had the face for it.

She wished now that she had called Julia before she left. Sara and Julia were seventeen the last time they had seen each other. Now they were in their 40s. Would Julia even recognize her?

Sara reached inside her purse for the loose photograph she had brought from home. She redirected the overhead light to study the image. It was the summer before their senior year at Beacon. Grady must have taken the photograph with the camera she and Julia had bought him for his birthday that year. He still used that old 35 mm. Sara had not, until then, attached a sentimental motive to his unwillingness to buy a newer model.

Sara returned the photograph to her purse and remembered the game she and Julia had invented in order to survive another boring summer in their small town. Julia would spin the globe on the desk in her bedroom, its blue world about the size of a basketball, attached to a rickety metal stand. The plastic earth rotated with dizzying speed and made waffling sounds as it turned, threatening to come off its manmade axis and bounce across the room.

Meanwhile, Sara would stand poised, eyes closed, ready to let fate decide their destination. Wherever her finger landed was the place they would be that day. With the help of National Geographic and the Encyclopedia Britannica, their imaginations soared to far-away possibilities.

When Julia had left, Sara's spinning world had halted. Now, almost thirty years later, she was finally having one of the adventures they had dreamed about. She was finally keeping her promise.

The businessman next to Sara snored, spittle forming at the corner of his mouth. Stubble had grown on his face overnight. They flew toward the rising sun. Flight attendants pushed their

carts down the aisle like bees dispensing honey, serving each passenger a beverage with a small plate of fruit, cheese, and pastry.
The businessman startled awake, looking over at Sara as if he had
found her lying in his hotel bed and had no idea how she had
gotten there. He quickly erased his drool, popped a piece of nicotine gum into his mouth and ordered a Bloody Mary from the
flight attendant.

The snow-covered Alps came into view, the morning sun re-
flecting off the snow. Sara pulled herself up straighter, and mentally took a picture of the scene before her. She thought of Julia's
spinning globe. Her finger had landed on the Alps. She smiled.

We must be getting close to Milan, Sara thought.

She went to the lavatory to wash her face. The tiny faucet re-
belled, splashing a wide ink-blot of water down the front of Sara's
blouse. She soaked up the water with midget sized paper towels
bracing her knee against the door to steady herself. She looked
like she had been in a fight with a garden hose.

Sara awkwardly applied fresh make-up, her elbow anchored
against the door. She dotted concealer on the gray arcs under her
eyes and blended it in. "Well, that's as good as it gets for now,"
she said. Sara relaxed her face and smiled at her reflection.

Who is that person? she thought. *She looks almost happy.*

Sara returned to her seat and shortly afterwards the jet began
its descent. The pilot spoke a few sentences, first in Italian, then
in English, telling them the time and weather in Milan and wishing
them a pleasant stay in Italy. Was she really going to Italy?

As a third grader she had done a geography report on Italy
citing their imports and exports, among other things, and drawing
a large map of the country that looked like a boot. Something

about it had captured her imagination, even then. I'll go there someday, she had thought at the time. It was as clear and tangible a thought as she had ever had.

"Could you please stop that?" the businessman said. They were the first words he had spoken to Sara the entire flight.

"Excuse me?"

He motioned to her hand. Without realizing it, Sara had been tapping her nails against the arm rest. A nervous habit she had indulged in since high school, when she had finally stopped chewing her nails and grown them out.

"I'm sorry, I didn't realize...."

He grunted and reached for an airline magazine in front of him.

"I'm visiting an old friend," Sara said. "Actually, I'm surprising her. She has no idea I'm coming to her art opening. But I guess I'm more nervous than I thought."

He turned a page, not looking at her.

"We haven't seen each other in almost thirty years," Sara continued, this time hoping to irritate him. She was nothing to him, a mere gnat whizzing around his head.

He turned another page. His disinterest did little to curb her excitement.

After a reasonably smooth landing passengers unloaded overhead compartments and began their migration through screening and customs. Like cattle directed through various chutes, they eventually ended up in baggage claim, where the same stream of rumpled passengers moved toward the exits. Outside the airport Sara was swept into a tide of activity. Animated Italians greeted loved ones. People stood like statues peering up at a large board of constantly updated flight information. The numbers and letters flickered past like a giant slot machine. She rolled her luggage out the front entrance and followed signs to the Autobus, which would take her to the train station.

I am in Italy, she kept telling herself. *This is an Italian expressway. This is an Italian billboard. We are passing Italians on their way to work.* Everything felt novel.

Fifty minutes later she had arrived at the train station. Despite Italy's consideration for the tourist trade, the station was confusing. On a website Sara had learned of pickpockets who preyed on befuddled tourists. At that moment she felt like the epitome of befuddlement.

Sara stood in a long line and bought a fare to Florence at the ticket counter from a helpful young man who spoke English. A loudspeaker constantly announced arrivals and departures in a language she couldn't understand. It took several seconds to decipher the track number from the electronic schedule and then Sara walked up the two flights of stairs to get to the tracks.

The family from the plane was ahead of her, the girl's hand securely in the hand of her mother. Sara felt like a child, too, at that moment. Someone who needed a hand to hold onto in such unfamiliar territory. She quickened her pace to catch up with them.

"Excuse me," Sara said to the father. "Are you going to Florence?"

"Yes, Firenze," he said.

"I am, too," Sara said, her excitement revealing her nervousness.

The crowd carried them along as they spoke.

"Have you been to Florence before?" the mother asked.

For the first time Sara noticed how young she was. Maybe just a little older than Jess.

"No, I haven't," Sara said. "It's my first trip to Europe."

"Oh, you'll love it," the father said. "This is Elizabeth's first trip abroad, too." He put a hand on his daughter's shoulder. She smiled at him. The man's hair was gray at the temples. He looked old enough to have grown children himself. Was this his second family? Sara wondered if Grady would get married again and start another family if Sara were out of the picture.

"Be sure and stamp your ticket," the man said to her.

Sara followed his lead and stamped her train ticket in the yellow box beside the tracks. They approached the train and she lifted her luggage up the steps. She had packed and repacked the bag to weigh less than 20 pounds as the websites suggested, but it was still heavy. The exertion triggered a twinge of tenderness underneath her blouse, stretching the scar that remained. In her excitement she had almost forgotten the cancer that had decided to return for a second act. But she challenged herself to put that aside for now and enjoy herself.

The family found their seats in the first section as Sara found her seat further back. The conductor made his way down the aisle. When he reached Sara he smiled, winked and validated her ticket without taking his eyes from hers. Were the stereotypes true? Sara wondered. She smiled and looked away.

The train traveled through the industrial section of Milan before entering the flat, Italian countryside. Buildings were the color of the land, made with stone. Terra-cotta roofs and balconies graced every apartment building. Farmhouses in the distance rested amidst green and brown patchwork squares of land, tilled for centuries.

They stopped in small towns where more people boarded and others departed. Sara took it all in, trying to imagine what it would be like to live there and ride the train to work or school. With every stop Sara was aware of getting closer to Julia.

Three hours later she arrived at the train station in Florence with luggage and jet lag in tow, she walked through the ornate train station out into the streets of Florence. Sara stopped and stood in the middle of the square taking in the ancient city around her.

I made it, she said to herself.

She smiled. In a rare moment, she felt proud of herself. She stood tall and breathed in the Italian air. Pigeons landed at her feet, as if she were a new statue to explore. When she moved, they cooed their surprise and flew away in unison.

Sara approached a taxi waiting near the train station. The driver quickly got out and lifted her luggage into the trunk. She showed him the piece of paper that confirmed her hotel and gave the address. He smiled and nodded. They traveled through the congested, narrow streets of Florence, sharing the road with an enormous number of scooters, Fiats, and pedestrians. The driver deftly maneuvered his way through the maze of streets and spoke like he drove, with very little pause. It hardly mattered that Sara couldn't understand a word. His monologue played in the background like a radio. Too excited and exhausted to fear for her life, Sara gripped the back seat and leaned into the corners of the cab with every curve.

A traffic light halted their progress. Sara caught her breath. The light changed. The driver accelerated quickly, swerving to miss a startled pedestrian. His dialogue became more animated, as Sara could only guess he held the pedestrian at fault.

Well, I wanted an adventure, she thought.

They took an immediate right before coming to an abrupt halt in front of a beautiful old hotel. The brass numbers on the outside matched the address on the paper she held in her hand. The driver pointed at the doorway and smiled. Despite the short, harrowing drive from the train station, he appeared completely devoid of stress. Sara gave him the appropriate euros and what she hoped was an appropriate tip. The driver thanked her, handed her luggage to the porter and drove away.

The photos on the internet had not done the hotel justice. It was exquisite. "Thank you, Mimi," Sara said under her breath. The room was spotless and filled with Italian antiques. She looked out her window that overlooked the Arno River.

Sara sat on the bed and took the invitation from her purse. She had four hours before Julia's opening. She had cut it close. Would Julia be happy to see her? At that moment she didn't really care. She set the alarm on her cell phone and lay down on the bed for a short nap. Within minutes sleep had finally claimed her.

It was dusk when the alarm went off and her jet-lagged body felt heavy when she rose. She showered and dressed in a simple black dress with a lightweight taupe shawl covering her shoulders, meant to hide the contours of her chest. Reconstructive surgery would have to wait until she returned, but for now she had pulled off looking halfway elegant.

Sara had the hotel call a cab and gave the driver the address on the invitation. This driver seemed in less of a hurry and Sara relaxed in the back seat. Florence was beautiful at night. Lights lit up large fountains in nearly every square. Balcony after balcony was filled with flowers and light.

The taxi arrived at the small gallery and she paid the driver and got out. For several seconds she stood outside taking a series of deep breathes, an exercise she taught her drama students to overcome stage fright. The gallery was crowded with people smiling and laughing and speaking a language Sara could not even begin to understand. The scene took on a surreal quality, considering that the day before she had been mopping floors, doing the laundry and sorting Grady's boxer shorts. She had wanted to leave the house in pristine condition in the event that her plane went down and she didn't return. It was her version of a mother's warning to wear clean underwear in the event of an accident.

Thinking of homemade Sara's new-found courage falter. She turned to look for the cab that had dropped her off. But the narrow street was empty. She peered through the window to try to catch a glimpse of Julia. A tall man, impeccably dressed, gestured for her to come inside. Sara smiled awkwardly and stepped into the gallery. He handed her a glass of wine from a nearby tray and said something to her in Italian.

She thanked him.

"Oh, you're American," the man said. His English was as impeccable as his manner. "Are you a friend of Julia's?"

"Yes, I am," Sara said.

He smiled. "She's in the back, greeting her admirers." He motioned to the back of the gallery.

"I guess I'll go get in line then," Sara said.

"By the way, I'm Roger," the man said. "I guess you could call me a friend, too."

"Nice to meet you, Roger." Sara smiled and held up her wine glass in a quick salute. "I'm Sara."

He bowed. "Nice to meet you, Sara."

The crowd in the back erupted in laughter. Sara caught a glimpse of the woman that stood in the center of the crowd. Past and present collided. Her heartbeat quickened a bit. All eyes were on her old friend as if she were a queen among commoners.

She hasn't changed a bit, Sara thought.

She asked Roger to excuse her and made her way toward the back. Everyone there was dressed in various renditions of black evening wear.

As Sara approached, she caught brief glimpses of the woman of the hour. Sara compared these glimpses to the girl she had once known. Her laugh was the same, as was her smile. Her long hair was pulled away from her face. Julia had always worn her hair long. Sara took a moment to run a hand through her short curls.

Sara was eight feet away but Julia's back was to her. She debated what to say. *Hi, Julia. Remember me?* Or maybe she should call her Jules, the nickname she had given her as a girl. She feared an awkward exchange as she remembered their phone call weeks before. If their meeting was a repeat of that phone call, Sara would be mortified; forced to climb under an Italian rock somewhere to hide her humiliation.

Sara stepped closer. She was close enough to smell Julia's perfume. Julia spoke to someone about her work, pointing to a canvas on the closest wall. Her Italian, from what Sara could tell was like a native and she appeared totally at ease in her surroundings.

What am I doing here? Sara thought.

She was totally out of her league. She was used to mingling with teachers and soccer moms, not artists and Florentine elite. Not to mention that she was a one-breasted cancer survivor. Survivor being a relative term. She glanced toward the entrance to plan her get-away. Thirty steps, maybe forty and she could be out of there. Sara turned toward the door just as Julia pivoted toward her. Their eyes met. Julia smiled to acknowledge her, a presumed stranger and possible admirer. But then her expression changed. Julia's smile widened. "Sara? Is that you?"

Chapter Six

Julia's smile evaporated any fear Sara had had about their meeting.

"Oh, Sara, what a surprise! It's so good to see you!"

"You, too," Sara said.

They embraced. *Had it really been nearly thirty years?* A scent of wildflowers permeated Julia's clothing and her hair. Sara breathed her in, as if taking a hit of oxygen after being depleted for years. Julia had aged, of course, but at the same time had become more beautiful. Was that even possible?

"I can't believe you came," Julia said.

She stepped back to look at Sara again. Julia took Sara's hand and Sara felt giddy; drunk with the knowledge that Julia was happy to see her.

"How did you get here?" Julia asked.

"The usual way," Sara said. She flapped her arms like wings and instantly blushed her embarrassment. "Sorry," she said. "I could get the Pulitzer for being lame these days."

"Don't be silly," Julia said. "I always loved your sense of humor."

Julia had not stopped smiling and Sara had to divert her eyes to withstand the attention.

"It means so much to me that you came," Julia said. "Is Grady here, too?" She quickly scanned the crowd.

"No, he's at home," Sara said.

Julia asked where she was staying and Sara told her. "Very up-scale," Julia said. "But I insist you stay with me. I have a great little place and then we'll have time to catch up."

The owner of the gallery apologized for the interruption and spoke to Julia.

"He wants me to meet someone interested in buying one of my paintings," Julia told her. "Don't go anywhere. We have so much to talk about."

Sara watched Julia be whisked away and turn on the charm with the potential buyers.

She could sell anything, Sara thought.

She had even sold Sara on staying with her. But this was something Sara didn't mind being sold on.

Sara walked around and for the first time studied the art on the walls. Julia's paintings were mostly abstract. Bold and with bright colors; lots of reds.

Some things never change, Sara thought.

Julia's paintings had an energy to them that felt like Julia: dynamic, compelling. Sara translated the prices on the paintings from euros to dollars. Could you really make that much money painting?

Too bad I can only draw stick figures, she thought.

Sara found a corner away from the crowd and observed the scene around her. She had never been around this level of sophistication. The women actually wore jewels. Sara suddenly felt tired. Considering how much sleep she had gotten these last few days, it was amazing that she could even stand. But none of this changed the fact that she was in Italy.

Several minutes later Julia reappeared with an elegant looking couple by her side. "Sara, I'd like you to meet my good friends Melanie and Max."

"Welcome to Italy," Melanie said. She greeted Sara with a quick kiss to each cheek. She was forty, at the most, and dressed in an elegant black pantsuit with short heels to match. She was almost as tall as her husband and slender.

"A pleasure," Max said. He extended his hand to Sara. A slight middle-aged paunch was evident underneath his black jacket, but otherwise he appeared tan and fit. Because of his dark hair and eyes he looked like an Italian businessman.

"Max and Melanie live in Siena," Julia said.

"But you're American, right?" Sara said.

"Yes," Melanie said. "Living in Italy is a dream come true for us. Thank God Max got in and out of tech stocks when he did. Or we might still be living in New Jersey."

Sara liked Max and Melanie instantly. She and Grady didn't have friends like this. They hardly had friends at all.

Roger approached and a look crossed Julia's face that Sara tried to decipher. Was she irritated with him? Or just slightly intolerant.

"Sara, this is Roger," Julia said. Her smile dulled.

"Yes, we met earlier," Sara said.

Roger's expression was slightly puppy-like, his gaze leaving Julia for only short amounts of time. Sara suddenly recognized the look. She had seen it on the faces of the high school boys that Julia had briefly dated. It was the look Julia's admirers got when they had been shown the door.

The evening was just getting started but to Sara it felt like the middle of the night. She made her apologies and announced her need to go back to the hotel. She had no idea if she were on New England time or Italy time. She felt like she was still hovering somewhere over the Atlantic Ocean.

"It's so nice to have met all of you," Sara said. "But it's been a long day."

Julia handed Sara a card with her address and phone number on it. "Check out of the hotel first thing in the morning," Julia said, "and come to my apartment for brunch. And I insist that you stay with me for the rest of your time in Florence, okay?"

"Okay," Sara said. Following Julia's lead, even after all these years, felt familiar to her and, at this moment, comforting.

"I'll get you a cab back to the hotel," Roger said, as he left Sara to say her goodbyes to Max and Melanie.

"Promise you'll come visit us," Melanie said. "We have a quaint little farmhouse on the Tuscan countryside."

Sara hesitated. Suddenly the whole trip was too much. Julia wanted her to come for brunch and then stay with her. Max and Melanie wanted her to visit. Since when had she gotten so popular? Julia had always had a knack for sweeping people along in her wake. Sara remembered that now. No wonder she had missed Julia so much after she had gone.

Roger returned to tell her a cab was waiting. Julia gave Sara a long embrace. "I'm so glad you're here," Julia said.

"Me, too," Sara said.

But this was the understatement of the year. Being in Italy felt crucial to her existence at this point. It gave her a B12 shot of hope. It didn't make sense, but somehow it felt like being in Italy was going to save Sara's life.

Chapter Seven

The next morning the taxi delivered Sara to the address on Julia's card. The large wooden door to the building opened just as Sara was reaching for the buzzer. An elderly couple stepped out of the building. The gentleman held the door for Sara and said something in Italian. She apologized for not understanding.

"Are you Julia's friend?" he then asked, in practiced English.

"Yes," she said.

"We are Julia's neighbors, the Baraldis," he said.

Sara shook his hand and curtsied to his wife like she had suddenly become Maria in *The Sound of Music* meeting Captain Von Trapp. The woman nodded regally and ignored Sara's awkwardness. Sara's eye was drawn to the cameo brooch of the Madonna and child adorning the collar of her dress.

"Julia is looking forward to your visit," Mr. Baraldi said.

Sara's relief spread into a smile. "I'm surprised she told you about it already. She only knew I was here last night."

"Of course," he said. "We saw her at the market early this morning."

"Your English is very good," Sara said to Mr. Baraldi.

He smiled and bowed slightly. His gray eyebrows and mustache were of equal thickness and a hint of gray tuft protruded from his ears. He had the kind face of a grandfather. He pointed to the stairway. "Third floor," he said. Sara thanked him and stepped inside.

A row of tall, thin mailboxes lined the wall just inside the door. On one of the boxes was an engraved nameplate that read *J. David*. A surge of anticipation chased away the exhaustion that had not quite left Sara since her flight. She ascended the stairway. The marble steps documented every footstep, their solidity slightly worn and shiny in the middle, as if a thousand pilgrims had made this trek over the last two centuries. Sara's wheeled luggage thumped loudly against each step.

She passed the second floor landing, and then reached the third. At the top of the stairs she glanced again at the Julia's card to make sure she was in the right place. Sara raised her hand to knock and stopped. What if their meeting didn't turn out as well as she hoped? She had forfeited her hotel room during the busy tourist season.

Sara took a deep breath and knocked lightly on the door. She waited. No one came. Several thoughts went through her mind at once. Had Julia forgotten she was coming? No, she had told the Biraldi's about it that morning. Did she knock too lightly? But then a latch released and the door opened. Julia greeted her with open arms and an embrace. Any hesitation Sara had felt quickly disappeared.

Julia wheeled her luggage into her apartment saying again how happy she was to see her.

"This is lovely," Sara said, seeing everything and nothing at the same time. A small gray cat appeared at her feet. "Who's this?" Sara asked.

"This is Roberto," Julia said.

Roberto rubbed his face against Sara's leg. "Can I pick him up?"

"You'd better check with him," Julia said. "He likes to make his own decisions."

"Hello, Roberto. May I hold you?" He raised his head, and Sara lifted him into her arms. Despite his cool demeanor, his heart beat rapidly underneath her fingertips.

"I'm impressed," Julia said. "He usually doesn't let strangers hold him right away. He must like you."

"I like him, too." After several affectionate rubs Sara returned Roberto to the floor.

"His sister is here somewhere, too," Julia said. "She's quite the shy one. A little afraid of life."

"I can relate," Sara said.

A smile had not left Julia's face since Sara had arrived. Sara suddenly wondered how she had managed to live this many years without seeing it.

"You haven't changed a bit," Julia said. "Of course, we're both a bit older."

"Just a bit," Sara said.

"Come in, come in," Julia said, leading the way into the living room.

Sara placed her handbag on a large, overstuffed chair near the entryway and followed Julia into the living room. The room was full of light. Large windows ran floor to ceiling and overlooked the rooftops of the city. A door stood partway open to a small balcony filled with flowering geraniums. The furnishings inside were antique, sophisticated, yet comfortable, accented with rich fabrics and colors. Sara was struck instantly by the absence of clutter. Yet Julia's apartment had warmth and a lived-in quality.

"It's beautiful," Sara said.

"I'll give you a quick tour, if you'd like," Julia said.

"I'd like," Sara said.

Julia showed Sara her kitchen where a rich assortment of eggs, fruit, and pastries awaited. The kitchen overlooked a courtyard with several small trees. Next was a small studio, which had a large blank canvas sitting on an easel close to the window, and then the bath, and the bedroom.

"I know it's small," Julia said. "But you wouldn't believe how expensive property is in Florence. There isn't much turnover, either, as you can imagine. I was able to get this for what a small mansion would cost in the States."

"Oh, I don't think it's too small at all," Sara said. "But are you sure my staying here isn't too much of an inconvenience?"

"Are you kidding?" Julia wrapped her arm around Sara's shoulder. "We must have had a million sleepovers when we were girls. Was that ever an inconvenience? The sofa becomes a bed, and I've been told it's very comfortable. We'll be fine."

"You're sure?"

"I'm sure," she said.

Julia directed Sara to the small terrace. From there they could survey Julia's little corner of Italy. Colorful laundry hung on clotheslines outside many of the windows. The scene could have been from a hundred years ago, if not for the small silver satellite dishes along the ancient roofs.

Sara took a deep breath, wanting to memorize the scene. She told herself not to cry. Just being in Italy had let loose a fountain of emotion and her eyes watered with this awareness.

The city appeared golden in the afternoon sunlight, the stone buildings baked to perfection for hundreds of years. Small clay pots of red geraniums lined the short black iron terrace, a perfect complement to the city. The fiery crimson of the flowers softened the look of the iron and stone. Julia had learned what Sara imagined Florentines had known for centuries: how to make the best of small, exquisite spaces.

Sara felt Julia watching her as she took in the scenery around them. Julia offered her a chair, one of two on the small terrace. Roberto joined them. He rubbed his whiskers against Sara's slacks to get her attention. She invited him up and he leapt gracefully into her lap. The sounds of the city were unusually hushed. An occasional scooter shot through the alley searching for a shortcut. Neighbors talked quietly in the street below. Small children played, and the bells of the nearby cathedral tolled three times.

"This is the most beautiful place in the world," Sara sighed.

Julia's smile widened. "I'm so glad you think so. I love it, too."

A smaller orange tabby appeared in the doorway, cautiously sniffing in Sara's direction. "Here's Roberto's sister, Bella," Julia said. "Come here, my shy little one." She wiggled a finger to entice her. For a moment Bella teetered at the cusp of the doorway. But then she backed away, into the safety of the living room.

"She lacks confidence," Julia said. "Unlike, my other little friend here." Roberto eyed a pigeon on a nearby rooftop, his tail swishing his primal desire.

"It's hard to believe I'm really here," Sara said, looking out over the city.

"How long can you stay?"

"Two weeks," Sara said, but she wanted to say forever.

"That almost gives us enough time to catch up," Julia said.

Julia's warm greeting had surpassed Sara's expectations. Italy was the dream of a lifetime but seeing Julia was more of a gift than she had realized. She still didn't know how much she would tell Julia about her current situation. Julia had no idea that Sara had, in essence, run away from her life back in the States and that the amount of time she had left of that life was also in question.

"Let's have brunch," Julia said. "Then I want to hear all about your life."

"There's nothing much to hear about," Sara said.

"Still the same old Sara." Julia smiled. "I used to have to pry things out of you. At one time I knew how to get you to open up. But I'm not so sure I remember anymore."

Sara followed Julia into the kitchen, remembering how natural it was to follow her lead.

Julia wore a long skirt and loose blouse, feminine and flowing, reds and purples fighting each other for attention. Artsy, some people would call it. She wore sandals with tethers that tied around her ankles. Julia was still beautiful and in her maturity had become elegant. Both things Sara felt she was not. She noted the difference in their clothing. Preferences carried forward from their youth. Sara's choices were subdued. Combinations of browns, grays, and blacks; nothing too exciting, or revealing.

Julia ground fresh coffee and turned on the kitchen faucet. The old pipes moaned softly, as if contemplating whether to deliver her request.

"Come on, you can do it," Julia coaxed the pipes. She glanced at Sara. "I think I need to find a new lover. I'm spending way too much time alone if I've resorted to talking to the kitchen sink." She laughed unapologetically.

Sara joined in the laughter. She had forgotten the ease to which Julia could make fun out of anything, even herself. A slow, steady stream of water flowed into the coffee pot. Julia hummed softly as she put the water on the stove to boil before pouring it in the carafe.

"I loved meeting your friends last night," Sara said.

"They loved meeting you. Melanie was serious about that invitation. And don't believe her when she says their place is 'quaint.' It's enormous and it's beautifully renovated."

"So who is Roger?" Sara asked, although she thought she already knew.

Julia grimaced slightly. "He's an architect, on business here in Florence. We met a few weeks ago and had a bit of a fling. But he ended up driving me insane. God knows what I was thinking. It must have been pure horniness."

Sara laughed. She had also forgotten how frank Julia could be.

"Some things never change." Julia winked as though reading Sara's thoughts.

"So what drove you insane?" Sara asked, hoping these were not traits she possessed.

Julia paused. "Am I allowed to be catty?" Sara nodded and Julia leaned close as if to tell Sara the most delicious of secrets. "For one thing he wore this little short terrycloth robe with his initials monogrammed on the right butt cheek. That's not something you buy yourself. Is it? I think he has a wife back in the States that he wasn't telling me about. And if that wasn't enough, he was absolutely paranoid that Roberto didn't like him. Roberto didn't, of course. But the man practically lost sleep over it."

"I guess that is *catty*," Sara said. "Pun intended." They laughed.

Julia took two cups from the glass-fronted china cabinet and poured them each a cup of the freshly brewed coffee and then gestured toward the food. "Shall we?"

Sara nodded.

After they filled their plates Julia led them into the dining room where two elegant place settings awaited, as well as crystal glasses of juice and water. Sara complimented Julia on how beautiful everything was, which Julia promptly waved away.

She continued on about Roger. How he wore his socks to bed and moved his lips when he read. They laughed at Roger's expense, which Sara felt mildly bad about. She had liked Roger when she had met him. But she had missed laughing. In fact, she couldn't remember the last time she had laughed this way. Laughter deep enough to make you ache, gasp for air and cross your legs all at the same time.

Sara also hadn't realized how much she had missed the sound of Julia's voice. The highs and lows of it, and its resonance. They finished brunch and took a second cup of coffee back to the terrace. Sara looked down into the courtyard. An old woman sat knitting on the steps at the back door of the building. She gestured for Julia to look.

"That's Mrs. Vinci," Julia said, "my friend Francesca's grandmother. She's been a widow since her husband was killed in Sicily in World War II."

"You're kidding," Sara said.

Mrs. Vinci looked up as if she had heard them. Julia waved and called out, "*Ciao*," which the old woman ignored. "She hates Americans," Julia said.

Directly across, Mrs. Baraldi walked out on their balcony, a laundry basket in her hands. Julia called the same to Mrs. Baraldi who responded in a lilting, singing greeting. She began to hang out laundry on their balcony, pinning the clothes to the small line with quick perfection, stringing up Mr. Baraldi's white jockey shorts like flags on the mast of a ship.

Mr. Baraldi opened the window above his wife and waved when he saw them. "Are you enjoying the reunion with your friend?" he asked Julia.

"Yes, very much, thank you," Julia answered.

"We met her downstairs," he said. He and Sara exchanged polite nods. Then he wished Sara a pleasant visit.

A floor apart, Mr. and Mrs. Baraldi conversed briefly in Italian before going back inside. Moments later they heard the clatter of dishes and a lively discussion when they reunited in the kitchen.

"Do you think they're talking about us?" Sara asked.

"About me, at least," Julia said. "I'm the strange American with no husband, two cats, and no job, at least as far as they can see. Someday I hope to understand the language well enough to catch them at it."

"They seem nice," Sara said.

"Oh, they're wonderful," she said. "I have been blessed with good friends and good neighbors."

The exhaustion in Sara's body was her only evidence that the scene wasn't a dream. She took a deep breath and relaxed into the chair on the terrace. It had taken her thirty years to arrive at the place she had dreamed about as a girl.

A rush of gratitude filled Sara as she realized the emotional and physical distance she had traveled to be sitting on Julia's terrace.

Chapter Eight

As the afternoon progressed Sara and Julia moved inside to the living room. Sunlight streamed through the side windows producing much better light than her home in New England with all the mature trees around it. Julia asked Sara about Grady and their children. Was it odd for her to imagine Sara with Grady? For years he wasn't someone either one of them would have considered romantically. He was their friend, of course, but also the guy they couldn't seem to get rid of.

Sara filled Julia in on her life in worded snapshots. Julia studied Sara as she spoke, as if the artist in her was taking in shape, shadow and light. Sara kept her eyes lowered; looking up only periodically to make sure Julia was still listening. Did she avoid eye contact when they were girls? She couldn't remember. Occasionally their eyes met before Sara looked away. Julia leaned closer, as though intent on capturing her gaze and locking it into place. But at that moment, Sara didn't want to be captured.

"I can't believe you work at Beacon High," Julia said.

"I teach English in Mrs. McGregor's old room."

"We had some good times in that room, didn't we? How is the old place?"

"The same, really," Sara said. "Too hot in summer; too cold in winter. A different generation of kids, but the same angst."

"I remember that angst," Julia said.

"You?" Sara asked. "You didn't seem to have a care in the world."

"You'd be surprised." Julia sipped her coffee, her long, slender fingers caressing the cup, her nails perfect, but unpolished. Two silver rings graced her right hand, one a simple wide band, the other quite ornate with a turquoise stone in the center. "I haven't been around teenagers since I was young myself."

"Lucky you." Sara laughed. "I had three teenagers in the house at the same time."

"I can't imagine," Julia sighed.

Roberto slid his body under Sara's hand.

"Watch out for him," Julia said. "He has the finesse of an Italian male."

"I wouldn't know," Sara said.

"I would," Julia smiled.

Sara caressed Roberto's head. He closed his eyes, as if perfectly content. Sara thought briefly of Roberto's disdain for Roger and felt pleased that he had accepted her.

Sara's thoughts wandered between past and present, bridging the years since she and Julia had seen each other. Julia was different, she decided, yet the same. Beautiful as ever; yet also older, less dependent on her beauty. And still the dominant force in a room. Was the girl she once was permanently imprinted on every woman?

"Tell me about you," Sara said. She wasn't ready to tell Julia about the cancer. If she told her at all. From her experience people changed once they knew. They developed an attitude of pity, peppered with relief that it hadn't happened to them.

"I wouldn't know where to begin," Julia said. She sat regally on the plush gold sofa, a queen presiding over her court. Even thirty years later Sara served at her pleasure.

"Your paintings are marvelous," Sara said. Had she told her that last night? If not, she had meant to.

"Thank you," Julia said. "It's hard to believe I'm painting again. I dabbled a little bit in high school, as you know. But then got lost in my career and didn't give it another thought until about four years ago."

"I wouldn't call what you did in high school 'dabbling,'" Sara said. "You won awards. You had an exhibit in the library our junior year."

"You remember that?"

"Of course," Sara said. "I've never told you this. But I was very proud to be your friend."

Julia leaned back and looked at her. "You were always so sweet, Sara."

Her face burned from Julia's compliment. Sweet? Had anyone ever called her sweet?

"I'm not sure why I gave up art," Julia began again. "Except that I needed to make money if I was going to go all the places I wanted to go. So I went to law school and worked in London for a number of years. Traveled all over Europe when I could get away, which wasn't often. But then at some point it just wasn't enough. I had to try the painting again or I would have always wondered. The great 'what if?' you know?" Julia paused thoughtfully.

Yes, Sara knew about the great 'what if?' She had been thinking about it a lot lately. *What if* Julia had never left Northampton?

What if they had gone away to college together like they had planned? Sara probably would have never married Grady nor had their children. But would she be happier?

"Now that I think about it," Julia began again, "coming back to painting was like being reunited with an old friend. Kind of like us."

Several seconds of silence passed. But not the kind of silence she was used to with Grady. This silence felt full instead of empty, pregnant instead of barren.

"Would you like to go for a walk?" Julia asked.

"I'd love to," Sara said. She welcomed a less intimate venue. Having Julia's undivided attention after so many years was exhausting.

"While we're out, I'll show you around a little bit," Julia said.

Sara grabbed her purse and Julia took keys off a hook near the door, calling goodbye to Roberto and the unseen Bella.

They walked down the marble steps. "Remember that cat you had when we were girls?" Sara asked. "I can't remember his name anymore. But half of one ear was missing."

"Oh, that was Vincent," Julia said. "I haven't thought of him for years." She paused on the dimly lit second floor landing, as if recalling the past. "Vincent had been in one cat fight too many, but he was a sweetheart. He lived to be some ungodly age, like twenty-one or something. He stayed with my parents after I left for college."

"Animals always loved you," Sara said. "At one point you had Vincent, the cat with one ear, and that poor dog that chased his tail until he fell over."

"That was Picasso," Julia laughed. "I can't believe there's someone in the world who remembers my childhood besides me. It's been years since I've thought of Vincent and Pico. I guess I was destined to be an artist if I named my pets such silly names."

"It wasn't silly," Sara said. "The names fit them perfectly."

Sunshine greeted them as they entered the street. Within seconds, the cathedral bells began to toll. Their foreign, sacred sound stopped Sara in the middle of the sidewalk.

"Oh, Julia, this is amazing."

"If you think that's amazing, just wait. We haven't even begun to reach amazing yet." She locked her arm in Sara's as they walked through the narrow streets of Julia's neighborhood. They crossed the Arno River into the main section of town. With Julia's leadership they moved through the crowds with ease. Sara observed her surroundings as if a camera documenting every frame. If this was her farewell tour, she was determined to make the most of it.

Julia squeezed her arm. "You act like someone who has been living off bread and water and is suddenly introduced to elegant food."

"You don't know how true that is," Sara said. She stopped and looked up at a building in the square. A relief of the Virgin Mary graced a stone shelf above a large wooden doorway. "From what I've seen so far, she seems to be everywhere," Sara said.

"She watches over the city," Julia said. "If you like this, there's a fountain at Max and Melanie's that you'll absolutely love."

They crossed a square to admire the famous doors of the Baptistery. The doors opened up into a glorious round room with a domed ceiling. Characters from the stories of Sara's childhood catechism classes looked down on them from every angle; classes that Sara had stopped when her mother died. Angels and saints in gold watched over the font where wealthy Florentines had baptized their infants. As Sara took in the gilded sight, Julia watched her.

"Relax Sara, you don't have to take it all in on this one trip."

But I do, Sara thought.

She had no idea of how to tell Julia that she might be dying. As long as she was in Italy she wanted to pretend that everything was all right. She had gotten good at pretending. Except that a part of her actually wanted to tell Julia the truth. When they had been friends they had always been truthful with one another, even if it hurt. If there was anyone Sara could be real with it was Julia. But did she even know what *real* was?

They crossed the piazza to the Duomo, a cathedral with one of the most famous domes in Europe. Sara had had a photograph of this dome posted on her wall as a girl. Before going to sleep, she would imagine herself there. And here she was! Her imagination could have never dreamed up how spectacular it was.

"You know, we just don't have anything like this in New England," Sara said.

Julia laughed. "You sound just like a tourist."

"I am a tourist. A glorious, grateful tourist."

"Well, I'm happy to be your guide," Julia said. "I doubt that home will ever be the same for you again."

"I wonder if that's good or bad," Sara said, as they walked inside.

"I guess you'll have to decide that for yourself," Julia said.

For several minutes she studied the ceiling of the Duomo. "Visiting Florence can be hard on a person's neck." Sara rubbed the evidence of this fact.

Julia's laugh echoed through the rotunda. Had she always loved Julia's laugh? she wondered.

"Tomorrow, we'll start on the art museums," Julia said. "First the Uffizi, then the Accademia to see Michelangelo's David."

"Are you sure you have the time? I can give myself the tour."

"I'm sure," Julia said. "But be aware that the sheer volume of art here can be overwhelming. You'll see lots of glassy-eyed tourists along the way. Then after you're totally saturated with art, we can take the train to Siena and visit Max and Melanie in the country. That should restore you completely."

The large, full tears that Sara had held in most of the day filled her eyes.

"What's wrong?" Julia said.

"Nothing's wrong," Sara said. "It's that everything's so right. Thank you," she added.

Julia took her hand. "For what?" she asked.

"For being here. For giving me a reason to come to Italy."

"It's my pleasure," Julia said.

Their eyes met and it was as if the thirty years that had passed since the last time they had seen each other had been erased.

Chapter Nine

Later that week, they departed the train station in Florence for Siena, a quick train trip to the south. "Are you sure they won't mind us coming?" Sara asked.

"I'm sure," Julia said. "Max and Melanie love it when people come to visit. They told me on the phone that they're really looking forward to it."

Sara observed the Tuscan countryside feeling pleasantly numb to its beauty. The last three days had been some of the best of her life. Her last hurrah, so to speak, was going well.

"I think you'll love Siena," Julia said. "They say that if Florence is the spirit of Italy, Siena is the soul."

"What a wonderful way to think about it," Sara said.

Their days together in Florence had been rich and full. Seeing the various highlights of the Renaissance had been an unexpected joy, and as Julia had predicted, a bit overwhelming. Yet Sara's world had expanded exponentially with each and every museum and excursion into the neighborhood. Home, indeed, would never be the same.

The train station in Siena was small and located on the outskirts of town. Their steps echoed on the platform.

"There they are," Julia said. She waved at Max and Melanie in the distance. "They insisted on picking us up. Wasn't that nice?"

"Very." Sara took a deep breath, suddenly nervous to meet Julia's friends again.

The attractive couple approached. "It's so kind of you to have me," Sara said to Max, shaking his hand.

"We're so glad you took us up on our invitation," Max said.

"How was your trip?" Melanie asked, as she gave both Julia and Sara a quick embrace.

"Perfect," Sara said.

"Then you approve?" Melanie asked, motioning as if the train station encompassed all of Tuscany.

"Yes, definitely," Sara said.

Earlier on the train Julia had described Melanie as perpetually perky. Yet this trait seemed to fit her as well as her outfit. It took ten years off her age, and was the only reason Sara might ever attempt perkiness herself.

"I must warn you," Max said. "Tuscany is easy to fall in love with."

"Well, I was head-over-heels just being in Florence," Sara said.

"She's not exaggerating," Julia said, as though pleased with her part in the love affair.

Max directed them to the car. As they walked, he wrapped an arm around Julia. "So what do you two want to do first?" he asked. "Shopping? Lunch? Home for a rest?" He loaded the trunk of a late model BMW with their suitcases.

"A short rest sounds good to me," Sara said. Today she had felt more fatigued than usual.

Julia glanced at Sara. Was she on to her? They traveled one of the most scenic highways in Tuscany yet Sara tightly clutched her bag.

Julia leaned toward her in the back seat. "Are you okay?" she whispered.

"I just can't believe everything that's happening," Sara said. "I haven't been anywhere and now I'm in Italy. It doesn't seem real."

"It's real," Julia said. "And I hope it's something you can get used to, because we've got a lot more to explore."

"Definitely," Sara said. "To be overwhelmed by beauty is a wonderful problem to have."

Julia looked at her. "Then why do you look so sad? Is there something you're not telling me? Are you and Grady all right?"

"We're fine," Sara said. Now wasn't the time to go into how unsatisfying her life was, especially the part that involved Grady. He hadn't called once while Sara had been there. Nor had she called him. A fact that Julia probably had noticed.

At the end of a long dirt driveway they pulled up in front of a large, renovated farmhouse. Its stone walls were the color of the earth, with dark wooden beams accenting the stone.

Not in the least bit 'quaint,' Sara thought, *more like spectacular.*

They went inside and Melanie showed Sara and Julia to the guest rooms. Sara's room overlooked the courtyard. The double windows were open wide and drew her toward the view below. It was like a secret garden, lush and luxurious. She put her bag on the nearby chair and breathed in the fresh air.

If anything could heal me, this could, she thought.

A large fountain graced the back wall of the garden, the fountain Julia had referred to earlier in her trip. A life-size statue of the Virgin Mary was the centerpiece of the stone fountain. The fountain was surrounded by robust plants in large, ornate containers. Water trickled from an opening in the wall behind the statue and created a pool at the virgin's feet.

I can't seem to escape her these days, she thought.

The Madonna was abundantly reproduced in paintings, tile work, and statuary in Italy. Not only in churches, but on neighborhood buildings, overlooking streets, parks, bridges, tunnels. In the States, she was practically nonexistent, lurking only in the dark corners of Catholic churches.

"It's beautiful here," Sara said, realizing both Melanie and Julia were watching her.

"We feel very fortunate," Melanie said as Max delivered their overnight bags from the car. "We'll leave you to settle in," Melanie added, "and Max will get busy fixing us some lunch for later."

"Must I do everything around here?" Max said.

Melanie playfully took his arm and led him out of the room. "Come on, you poor man. You have such a rough life." He whimpered for their amusement.

After Max and Melanie left, Julia and Sara were alone in the room. "I hope they aren't too much for you," Julia said.

"Your friends are perfectly wonderful," Sara said. "But I am a little tired."

"Are you sure you're okay?" Julia asked.

"Sure," Sara said.

"Max and Melanie are two of the most genuinely accepting people I've ever known," Julia said. "So don't feel like you have to be a certain way in front of them. Just do whatever you need to do. We can have a very low key visit, if you'd like."

"That's very thoughtful of you," Sara said.

"Not thoughtful, I just don't want you to do something you don't really want to do."

"Well, that's a change," Sara smiled. "When we were girls, you had me doing all sorts of things I didn't want to do."

"Like what?" Julia appeared genuinely curious.

"Let's see . . . you had me trying out for cheerleader, even though I was a total klutz. And then we joined the marching band because you had a crush on that hunky drum major and wanted to sit with him in the back of the bus on band trips. You even talked Grady into jumping off the high board at the Y. Remember when his swimming trunks fell off when he landed? He won't get on a high board to this day."

Julia laughed. "I suppose I was a little overbearing."

"A little?"

"I've changed," Julia insisted, not looking the least bit repentant.

"Don't worry. I always loved you anyway."

"Well, that's reassuring, at least." Julia gazed at the courtyard below. "It's beautiful, isn't it?"

"Absolutely," Sara said. They stood for several seconds admiring the view. "Get some rest," Julia said, before turning to walk away, "and I'll see you in about an hour?"

"An hour," Sara repeated.

Julia disappeared into the guest room next door. Despite the thickness of the doors and walls, Sara could hear Julia's every move because of the open windows. She listened for a long time, imagining the movements that went with the sounds: luggage unzipped, drawers opening and closing, the closet door echoing the drawers.

Everything in Sara's room was an antique and appeared to be carefully chosen to match the period of the farmhouse. A large brass bed dominated the center of one wall, adorned with an ornate quilt, luxurious, yet homey.

Sara hung up the outfit she planned to wear that evening and gazed down at the courtyard again. The eternal Mary in stone, her arms outstretched, embraced the garden. Sara was intrigued by her. The expression on her face, at least from this angle, appeared to be longing. Sara related to this feeling and suddenly felt tired and lay on the bed.

An hour later she freshened up in the bathroom upstairs and then joined Julia and Max in the kitchen.

"How was your rest?" Max asked her. He was preparing a pasta and bean salad in a large ceramic bowl.

"Wonderful," Sara yawned.

"I think her trip to Italy has been a bit overwhelming so far," Julia said.

"But in a good way," Sara said, stifling another yawn. Max and Julia laughed. Max seemed more at home in his kitchen than Sara had ever been in hers. "Where's Melanie?" Sara asked.

"At the neighborhood vineyard, getting some wine," he said.

"Melanie's very lucky to have her own personal chef," Julia said.

"You're quite the chef yourself," Max said to Julia. "Sara, did you know your friend is a marvelous cook?"

"We had a wonderful brunch a few days ago. Other than that we've been eating out every night. But I do remember that when we were girls she could make a great grilled cheese sandwich."

"I was an expert at peanut butter and jelly, too," Julia said.

"Made with strawberry preserves," Sara reminded her. "You had this thing for red. Orange marmalade would never do."

"How do you remember that?" Julia laughed.

"It's funny," Sara said. "I seem to remember more about you than I do about myself."

"Well, maybe we can talk Julia into cooking for us while you're here," Max said. "Peanut butter and jelly sandwiches will be fine."

"I'm sure I can come up with something a little more interesting," Julia said.

The gentle gurgling of the fountain floated through the double doors which opened out from the kitchen into the garden.

"Would you like to go into the garden?" Julia asked Sara.

"I'd love to," Sara said. They walked outside, down several large, wide stone steps. Terra-cotta pots lined each step, the lush greenness of the plants accenting the lighter stone of the surrounding wall.

Adjacent to the fountain was an inviting wooden bench. The statue, almost the same height as Sara, reigned over the entire garden.

"After living in Europe all this time, you'd think I'd be immune to icons," Julia said. "But this one touches me for some reason. I think it's because she seems so totally at peace in her surroundings."

Sara couldn't imagine being that peaceful. They sat on the bench across from the fountain. The fountain trickled a steady accompaniment to their silence.

"This is an amazing garden," Sara said finally. "The only thing I grow really well in my garden at home is weeds." Her half-hearted laugh died quickly.

"I had a dream about you the other day," Julia said.

"Really?" Sara said. This intrigued her.

"It had something to do with this fountain." Julia paused as if to retrieve the details.

"You were sitting right over there, at the Virgin's feet." She pointed and then smiled as if remembering more.

"I love that you dreamed about me here." Sara walked over to the edge of the fountain near where Julia had seen her in the dream and dropped to her knees. She let her fingertips fall into the water. Her hand swept the gentle currents as water rippled outward. "Several times since I've been here," Sara said. "I've felt like I've dreamed it before. Kind of like déjà vu. Do you believe that's possible?"

"It seems as plausible as anything else," Julia said.

For several seconds they watched the fountain. Then Julia turned to watch her. "You're so beautiful sitting there," Julia said to Sara. "It's like you and the woman in the fountain belong together."

Sara turned away, hiding the pleasure she felt by this remark. Did Julia call her beautiful?

"I guess I do believe in déjà vu," Julia continued, "because the scene is almost exactly what I dreamed. The only difference was that in the dream, you took a handful of water and poured it over your head, like you were baptizing yourself."

"Well, let's do this right, then," Sara said. She raised her face to the woman in stone and scooped up a handful of water. Then she tilted her head back and let the droplets fall on her forehead. "Like this?" she asked. She would have done anything for Julia at that moment.

When Sara turned back to see if Julia approved, the expression on Julia's face was one she had never seen before. She looked both curious and pleased, as if she was seeing Sara for the first time.

Yet something about the look made Sara feel uncomfortable. She was used to being invisible; now Julia had seen her. At the same time something about this moment made everything she had been through in the last year feel worthwhile and she would have been willing to go through it all again if it meant she would end up in this same place.

Chapter Ten

Sara wiped the water from her face and then wiped her hands on her pants. "Grady would think I've gone nuts," she said, wondering why she would choose to bring up Grady at that moment, except that the thought of him was guaranteed to sober her.

"Grady always was a little too predictable for me," Julia said. "Sorry," she added, as though she realized she was talking about Sara's husband.

"No, it's true," Sara said. "He's still like that. But what's sad is that I've been that predictable too, Jules."

"I haven't heard that name in thirty years."

"Sorry," she said.

"No, I love it. It's the only nickname I've ever had."

A bird flew in and sat on one of the open arms of the statue. Sara thought again of the sparrows in the home improvement store. She was one of them and she had gotten away.

"I wonder if she finds us humorous," Julia said, looking up at the Madonna. "We worry about such trivial things."

"Like noses," Sara said, running a finger along the slight crook. "I hate to think of how much time I've wasted hating my nose."

"You have a great nose," Julia said.

"You've always said that. But best friends lie, don't they?"

"Not about the important things." They laughed with the lightness of girls.

"You're different somehow, from when you first arrived," Julia said.

"Because I'm baptizing myself in fountains?"

"No, I mean you seem more relaxed. You have a vitality I haven't seen before."

My oncologist would be happy to hear that, Sara thought, but didn't speak it.

For the first time since she had been in Italy she actually wanted to tell Julia the truth. But she didn't want to ruin the moment.

Water trickled a steady stream out of the stone wall. "Life just keeps going, doesn't it? With or without us," Sara said. "These statues will still be standing long after we're gone."

"Well that's philosophical of you," Julia said.

"I've been thinking lately about my mother," Sara said. "I know it's silly, but I still miss her and it's been decades."

"You always were very sensitive, Sara. It's one of the things I love about you."

"There's more than one?" Sara laughed. "To be honest, I always wondered why you were my friend."

Julia leaned back on the bench, a slight look of surprise on her face. "Oh, Sara," she sighed. "You haven't really changed much at all, have you? You don't get who you really are."

"Who am I?" Sara asked, as if she had been waiting her whole life to hear.

Julia leaned closer. "You are a beautiful, sensitive, caring, self-effacing, funny soul," Julia said.

"Truthfully?"

Julia nodded. "And I don't know what I would have done without you when we were growing up," Julia continued. "I was so lonely, you know? I was an only child with two intellectual parents. You were like a sister to me or a soul mate. We could talk about anything. We laughed constantly. Not to mention that you put up with me, for God's sake. I must have been the bossiest little girl on the planet."

Julia paused as a bird took a bath on the edge of the fountain. Sara and Julia smiled at each other as they watched.

"Thanks for saying all that," Sara said. "It means a lot to me."

Actually, it meant more than Julia would probably ever know, Sara thought.

"I can't believe you never knew how I felt about you," Julia said. "So much goes on underneath that calm exterior of yours. What else are you not telling me?"

"Can we take a walk?" Sara asked. She stood.

"Now I *know* there's something you're not telling me."

"Not now," Sara said softly.

"Okay, I'll drop it," Julia said. "But I'm here whenever you get ready."

Sara nodded.

They walked through the courtyard gate and up a dirt path toward a hill. This place was as different from New England as Sara could imagine. But 'different' had been exactly what she needed.

"It feels good to move," Sara said. "If we'd stayed at the fountain any longer I may have become stone myself." Sara felt closer to Julia since their talk. Was she really all those things that Julia said? She hoped so.

Julia led them through an acre of olive trees, followed by a large field planted with sunflowers, their green stalks just beginning to break through the ground. In a matter of weeks their blossoms would be like praying hands reaching toward the sun. The beauty of the Italian countryside elicited a lightness in Sara's chest. She briefly touched her scar and turned her face toward the sun, soaking in its rays like the new shoots of the flowers.

At the top of the hill they looked out over a large slice of Tuscany. A man on a tractor plowed a field on a square of earth in the distant valley below. Another figure rode a motor bike, releasing a ribbon of dust down the long driveway beyond the field. Green, yellow, and brown squares formed a patchwork quilt of earth in front of them.

"What do you think?" Julia asked.

"Heavenly," Sara said.

Julia spontaneously hugged her. The genuineness of Julia's gesture caught Sara off guard. She hesitated before returning the embrace. And then didn't want to admit how much she had wanted it.

"I didn't realize how much I missed you," Julia whispered in her ear.

At that moment the beauty of everything around her, including Julia, expanded Sara's chest and threatened to burst open the scar. Italy was bringing Sara back to life. But maybe that wasn't such a good thing.

Sara suddenly felt confused. Mixed with the confusion were feelings she had never experienced before, except with Grady after they had first been married. It was as if all the lines she had drawn until now were blurring. Was she falling for Julia?

Sara turned toward the path, wanting to run away. She wanted to be home. Home with Grady; Luke, the dog; her uninspired students; and everything predictable and familiar. Things were too foreign here, including the new emotions waking up in her.

"Is something wrong?" Julia asked.

"I'm ready to go back," Sara said. She hated how cowardly she felt.

"What is it?" Julia asked.

"Nothing," Sara said. She wasn't about to admit to Julia something she couldn't even admit to herself.

They returned to the house through another field of sunflowers surrounded by a patch of gnarled olive trees. A painter's paradise, Sara decided. Actually, anyone's paradise. For the rest of the walk she kept her eyes focused on the path in front of her, fielding the thoughts and feelings she couldn't put words to yet. Julia, who seemed to know instinctively that Sara needed space, didn't speak on their return. When they entered the courtyard through the gate, Sara averted her eyes from the woman in stone, imagining she could read her mind, as well as her heart.

"There they are," Melanie said when they entered the kitchen. "We'd almost given up on you."

"We took a walk," Julia said. "Up to the summit."

"How lovely," Melanie said.

A large earthenware bowl of pasta sat next to a mixed green salad on a large antique wooden table in the dining room. Bread and wine balanced out the feast. For the first time Sara noticed the ice pick that stood erect in the center of the table next to a vase full of flowers. It appeared to have a permanent mooring there, next to an assortment of signatures carved into the wood.

"Former owners of the table and their family members," Max said, answering Sara's unasked question. "We've continued the tradition. All our family and friends sign it. Before you leave, I hope you'll do us the honor."

Somehow leaving her mark on an old table in Italy touched her deeply. Tears threatened to wash over every name, the flow as unending as the fountain outside. Sara took a sip of water to prevent the outpour. One of the newest carvings was Julia's. Sara instantly wanted to add her name next to Julia's and encircle it with a primitive heart: *S.S. + J.D.* She shook the thought away.

Sara offered a sentence or two through the rest of the meal but didn't feel like talking. After all those years of holding herself together she was finally losing it. Exhilaration and terror mingled with the bread and wine. The ground was dissolving underneath her. She was between worlds. Instead of a near-death experience, she was having a near-life one. At that moment death seemed easier. Life was too messy and unpredictable.

Sara faked a headache and returned to the safety of her room. The door locked, she curled up on the bed, gripping her knees, wanting to cut off the oxygen to the emotion. *You're losing it,* the critical voice in her head reminded her.

Shut up! Sara thought, and for once the voice seemed to listen.

Pull yourself together, she coached herself. *A week from now you'll be home. Back to normal life. For now, just go with it.*

Sara breathed deeply, taking her own advice. After a few minutes she got up in search of something normal to do.

Post cards, she thought.

She had bought dozens of postcards and not sent a single one. She sat at the small antique desk next to the window to write, hoping this ordinary, mundane action would center her in her ordinary, mundane life.

The late afternoon sun peaked through the lace curtains billowing softly in the wind. She wrote a post card to each of her children and to her friend Maggie at school. Multiple renditions of: *The Tuscan countryside is beautiful. Wish you were here.* The characteristically trite message was nothing compared to the reality of the experience. She debated whether to send one to Grady and decided against it. She didn't wish he was here in the least.

Julia entered the room next to Sara's. Every creak in the floors of the old farmhouse revealed her presence. The windows opened. Then the faint squeak of her bed told Sara she was resting. Funny, she had never thought of Julia as needing rest. Her vitality was steady, unquestionable, and as unending as the fountain outside. Yet she had to expand the version of Julia she had kept locked in her memory all these years. Desire had never been part of it.

Sara stacked the post cards neatly on the corner of the desk and returned to the bed to rest. The box springs responded to her every movement. Was Julia listening to her, too? As girls, they would have jumped on a bed like this. Sara would have been cautious, as always. Unlike Julia, who would not have stopped until she had propelled herself upward and touched the ceiling or a grownup showed up at the door.

Sara closed her eyes and took inventory of her body, an action guaranteed to distract her. Besides a mild headache that had just started, her calves and thighs ached slightly from all the walking they had been doing. Before Sara's diagnosis, she didn't always notice the aches. But now she noticed everything. Every twinge could be an announcement of the cancer taking reign over a major organ or a lymph node.

Her composure began to unravel again as her thoughts returned to when she and Julia were at the summit. She tried to remain reasonable and understand what had happened. Somehow the beauty there, coupled with her desire to experience life fully, had led to feelings for Julia. Had Julia realized what was happening? She buried her face in her pillow to smother her embarrassment and shame.

Chapter Eleven

The next day Julia had to return unexpectedly to Florence on business. Another dealer was there for the day and wanted to see her work. Sara had insisted it was no problem. And in fact, it wasn't. She welcomed a day to have to herself so she could recover from the intense feelings from the day before. Sara borrowed Max and Melanie's car to drop Julia at the train station and then planned to spend the day in Siena on her own.

Sara roamed through a few shops enjoying her independence. She was proud of herself for exploring this beautiful city on her own. She wandered into another dress shop and was drawn to a display of scarves. She picked up a red silk one and caressed her face. At first she considered buying the scarf for Julia. But then she wondered if she might buy it for herself.

A young woman about Jess' age walked over and showed Sara how to arrange the scarf to accentuate her neck. When Sara looked in the full-length mirror she hardly recognized herself. The scarf brought out the color in her cheeks and made her face look alive. She paid for the scarf, oscillating between pleasure and guilt for the purchase, and wore it out of the store. She felt conspicuous at first, as if she had a red target around her neck. But then she began to relax into this new look. A few men smiled at her and she realized she was smiling back.

On the next corner she went inside a small café and chose a table near the window. She decided to rest awhile and people-watch. She placed her purse in the chair next to her and an attractive young waiter walked toward her.

"Good afternoon, Madam. Can I get you something?" he said in broken English.

Two things concerned her immediately. First, how did he know she was American? And second, was a woman in her 40s already a madam? The word sounded matronly. Grady's mother was a madam. Not Sara. Then she entertained the gruesome thought that he was about the same age as her sons.

"I'll have a cappuccino," she said. Sara looked briefly into his dark, Mediterranean eyes and was reminded of the statue of David by Michelangelo that she had seen in Florence. His features were smooth, classic, and other-worldly. A spark of attraction erased some of her confusion from the day before. She smiled her relief.

He bowed slightly, as if the smile was for him, and left to get her order. Behind the counter the clatter of cups and saucers competed with the assertion of the espresso machine. Minutes later, the young waiter returned carrying a cappuccino and two short-bread cookies on a small saucer. She started to tell him he had made a mistake with the cookies but he stopped her and said, "A gift, Madam."

Sara thanked him and smiled. The young man returned a brief smile before lowering his eyes and leaving again. Was he flirting with her? She found this hard to believe. No one had flirted with her since her first child was born.

An older gentleman sat at an adjacent table and tipped his hat to her before placing it on the table. It was odd to get this much attention.

Maybe this is what it's like to be Julia, she thought.

Everyone turned to look at Julia. As much now as they had in high school. Despite Julia's assertions, that kind of beauty had never been one of Sara's assets. In high school she was thought of as "cute."

Sara glanced across the café. Across the room the young waiter served a couple with their new baby. As soon as he finished with them he came over to fill her water glass.

"Is everything satisfactory, Madam?"

"Perfect," Sara said. She smiled, feeling oddly romantic. Was she really fantasizing over a waiter half her age? She reveled in the thought that she was normal after all. She could now dismiss the feelings for Julia as too much Tuscan sun.

Sara smiled her relief and took in the experience of Siena. Flowers were everywhere—in parks, in front of buildings, adorning window boxes. The café smelled of fresh bread, pastries and espresso. If the waiter wasn't enough to make her salivate, the aromas coming from the kitchen were. The town's buildings were actually the color of sienna, with green shutters on every building. Colorful flags representing the different neighborhoods adorned every street.

The light seemed different in Tuscany. Brighter, more alive. A group of students with sketch pads were set up on the corner to capture the architecture in their drawings. The clatter of dishes echoed in the back room of the café. Sara looked around for the young waiter who was nowhere in sight. Music floated in from the street corner. Even accordion music sounded romantic here. The musician played a tarantella, then *Hello Dolly*, perhaps to attract tips from American tourists.

The feeling in Europe was totally different from what Sara had experienced in the States. In America there was still the sense of the frontier. A town was considered historic if it had been in existence for a hundred years. In Italy, buildings had been standing for many centuries. Layers of history dwelled on every city block. Walls surrounded the city, with tracts of farmland inside, so that when medieval enemies attacked, the city could be self-sufficient.

The young waiter returned again and this time brought Sara a bowl of fresh strawberries. "Are you sure you won't get in trouble with your boss for this?" she asked, motioning toward the strawberries.

He leaned closer and smiled. "I am the owner," he said. He winked at her and bowed again.

Sara's face reddened to the color of the strawberries. The waiter hesitated before walking away and then turned to look directly at her. "I take a break soon. Would you take a walk with me?"

"Pardon?" Sara asked.

He started to repeat himself but she stopped him. "I'm sorry, I heard you. I just didn't expect you to say that." His expression turned from hopeful to confused. "Have I insulted you, Madam?"

"No, you've flattered me, actually. It's just that I'm married."

He shrugged, as if this were a minor detail. "I was just suggesting a walk," he said. "My name is Antonio." He extended his hand for her to shake. It was warm and slightly sweaty.

A moment of awkwardness followed.

What harm would a walk do? she thought.

She agreed and Antonio smiled and excused himself. When he returned his apron was gone and he was wearing a white shirt with an open-necked collar that revealed a chest full of dark hair. Nestled within the forest of hair was a gold medallion of the Virgin Mary. Sara averted her eyes so she wouldn't stare. She couldn't seem to get away from the holy virgin these days. But she was certain she was the only virgin between them.

Antonio held the door open for her as they walked out into the streets of Siena. They immediately settled into a stroll that would have gotten them plowed down by other pedestrians if they were in the States.

"What brings you to Italy?" he asked.

"I'm visiting an old friend," Sara said.

"Man or woman?"

"A woman. We were girls together."

"Why is your friend not here with you?"

"She had to go into Florence today for business."

"Pity," he said. "Is she as beautiful as you?"

Sara smiled and touched the scarf around her neck. Even if it was just a line she loved it. They continued to walk, avoiding the occasional bicycle. When they reached Il Campo, the city square, they stopped. It was a sunny day, in the low 70s. A sea of people had washed up on the sandy stonework. Tourists mingled with locals, who ate their lunch and soaked in the sun.

"It's beautiful here," she said, a line she had found herself saying or thinking frequently while in Italy.

He nodded, as if proud of his home. "I have lived here my entire life," he said.

"Do you ever think about living somewhere else?" she asked.

"Never," he said. "I love it here."

Sara couldn't imagine what it was like to live somewhere that you loved.

They took a narrow side street and stopped to watch a cobbler repairing a shoe in his small shop. The door was open wide, letting the fresh air inside. The old man sat on a stool at a wooden table. Dozens of pairs of shoes and boots hung on wooden hooks along the wall. Antonio waved to the old man, who returned the wave.

"He's been doing that for fifty years," Antonio said. "Following in the footsteps of his father and grandfather."

"I read somewhere that the average American changes jobs seven times," Sara said.

"Is that true?" he asked.

Sara nodded.

"That is very different from here," he said.

They began to walk again and took another turn into a more residential area.

"Would you like to see where I live?" Antonio asked.

His expression was innocent enough, Sara thought, *even if his intention was not.*

Sara hesitated. She didn't know who she was anymore. She was walking through Siena with a man who was a stranger only an hour before, contemplating going to his apartment. Was this somehow the anti-venom to being physically attracted to her best friend?

She was a woman in her 40s who had only slept with one person her entire life. That was practically archaic these days. Did a person like her sleep with total strangers? Of course, he hadn't exactly asked her to do that. But why else would he ask her to see where he lived? Did he want to show her his infamous etchings?

They climbed the narrow steps to Antonio's small fourth floor apartment. With each step she analyzed the situation. She had never been unfaithful to Grady. She had never even fantasized about being unfaithful.

But what better way to pull yourself from the edge of extinction, she thought, *than having a romp with a beautiful Italian man in Siena.*

Antonio opened the door to his apartment and the air went out of Sara's fantasy. Dirty dishes were stacked high in the sink. Clothes pungent with perspiration lined the floor. In contrast to the enormous mess, the most resplendent feature of the room was the bed. It was positioned directly in front of a large window and appeared to possess clean sheets, a fact she found both disturbing and heartening.

Antonio walked across the room and opened the window. Fresh air chased away her second thoughts. She stepped over a mound of dirty clothes to look outside. Life was abundant on the street below. Plants in terra-cotta pots crowded the window boxes. Pigeons had built nests in the porticoes. The smell of sautéed garlic rose from a lower apartment. With the breeze and the sounds of life outside, Sara inhaled deeply, as if she had been invited to make love to the city itself.

Antonio stepped closer. Within seconds his tongue was probing Sara's mouth. She tried to forget about the dirty, sweaty laundry brushing up against her ankles. A faint taste of garlic traveled on his breath and Sara wondered briefly if Antonio had a girlfriend who would arrive later and cook his dinner. Or perhaps even a mother. Antonio deftly removed her scarf and tossed it on another mound of dirty white shirts on the back of a chair. Then he unbuttoned the top button of her blouse.

"Wait!" Sara said.

Antonio jumped slightly, as if she had scared him. In her re-inventing of herself she had forgotten the pink elephant in the room: she only had one breast. She imagined him horrified or disgusted by this fact. Or like Grady, he may just pretend the scar wasn't there. At any rate, it was something she had not planned on.

Antonio watched her, a coy smile on his face. "Is there something bothering you?"

"I can't," Sara said. "My friends are waiting for me." Sara buttoned the top of her blouse, grabbed her scarf from the back of the chair and retied it. Then she stepped over the clothes to an island at the door where she could actually see the floor.

"But we were having such a good time," Antonio smiled.

"The walk was wonderful," Sara said, "and you've been very sweet, but . . . ."

"But what?" He reached out to her, the Virgin Mary swinging briefly before nestling back into the fur of his chest.

"I'm sorry, but I have to go," she said.

Antonio followed Sara down the stairs and they walked without speaking to the central parking lot where Sara had left Max and Melanie's car.

"Did I do something wrong?" he asked, as she unlocked the car.

He suddenly seemed much younger. "No," Sara said. "It's just not a good time."

"I'd like to see you again," he said. The afternoon sun revealed the perfection of his twenty-something skin.

"I know where to find you," Sara said. Did she really say that? His dejected look prompted her to kiss him on the cheek before getting into her car. He stuck his hands in his pockets and watched her as she drove away.

Sara followed the road back to Max and Melanie's and turned down their long dirt and gravel driveway. Her thoughts were still reeling from the events of the day when she parked and walked through the courtyard. She stopped at the Madonna in stone and smiled remembering the gold necklace dangling from Antonio's neck. Sara placed her hand in the stone virgin's upturned palm, as if to pay homage to the earthy deity. "Are you the one responsible for all this craziness?" Sara asked thoughtfully. But at least there were no witnesses to her most recent debacle.

Sara was already doing things in Italy that were totally out of character, as her daughter Jess would say. But how far was she willing to go with this exercise in character development?

Chapter Twelve

Later that evening Sara dressed for dinner. Her usual earth-tone outfit was set off by the red scarf that she had purchased in Siena. Sara looked in the mirror and arranged it the way the young woman in the dress shop had shown her and pronounced herself ready.

Sara joined everyone downstairs and Max handed her a glass of wine. Julia had returned and had good news. A gallery in Rome was interested in her paintings. She told them all the details and they toasted to her success.

"What a beautiful scarf," Julia said, as they moved from the living room to the dining room. Julia fondled the folds of the silk. Sara had done her best to not get too close to Julia for fear that she would discover that she was still attracted to her.

"I can't believe I bought something so bold," Sara said.

"Bold suits you," Julia said.

Sara glanced at Julia, smiled, and then looked away.

Bold can get a person in trouble, she thought.

She remembered Antonio's apartment and shuddered slightly.

They had an exquisite dinner in the large dining room and then returned to the living room, another glass of wine in hand. That made three glasses in the last hour and a half and she was beginning to feel it. She and Julia sat on opposite ends of a large sofa. The evening had cooled and there was a small fire in the fireplace.

"So when was the last time you two saw each other?" Max asked.

"When I was sixteen, my father got a teaching job in England and we moved away," Julia said.

"Our little town hasn't been the same without you," Sara said.

"I haven't been the same without our little town," Julia said. "I felt really bad about leaving."

"Did you?" Sara asked. For some reason Sara had never considered that the move would have been hard for Julia.

"Of course," Julia said. "I was heartbroken. I was leaving my best friend."

Max opened another bottle of wine and filled Sara's glass again. "This one was a gift from friends who own a vineyard to the north of us. I think you'll like it."

Sara thanked him, loosened her scarf, and took off her shoes. She slid her feet up under a sofa cushion, a gesture that would be more typical of Julia than her. The small fire crackled in the stone fireplace. Max and Melanie were easy to be with, as easy as Italy was to visit. Despite a few moments of terror, Sara was starting to relax here. Maybe a little too much.

A surge of heat rose to her face, followed by a mild panic, which historically announced the beginnings of a full-fledged hot flash. Sara made her apologies and exited to the garden. She took off her scarf and unbuttoned the top two buttons on her blouse.

Seconds later, Julia joined her. "Are you okay?" she asked.

"A menopausal moment, I think." Sara fanned herself with her scarf. The sky was clear, overrun with stars; the night air crisp, yet still. The three-quarter moon lit up portions of the courtyard.

"You seem awfully young to be getting hot flashes," Julia said.

"Thank you for that," Sara said.

The light from the house cast window-sized rectangles on the stone courtyard. The fountain, in the shadows, gurgled its constant presence.

Sara dropped her scarf on the bench. It had gotten her in enough trouble for one day. Her heartbeat accelerated. She rolled up the sleeves of her blouse, dabbing at the sweat forming in the valley of her chest.

"I haven't had one of these in a while," Sara said. "It's probably the wine. I never drink this much."

"What can I do?" Julia asked, concern in her voice.

"Nothing. I think it's almost over." Sara walked through the shadows and sat next to the fountain. She patted her neck with cool water, as if it were an elixir for what troubled her. The flash of heat made a crescendo and then faded away. She began to feel normal again and offered Julia a faint smile.

Sara looked up into the night full of stars that had no city lights to detract from them.

"Star light, star bright," Sara began.

Julia smiled her recognition. "Do you have a wish?"

Sara closed her eyes. She rejected the first wish that came to her, which was to stay in Italy forever. Her second wish was more in line with the *old* Sara. "Yes, I have one," Sara said, opening her eyes.

"Wait," Julia said. "We need to do this right." Julia took Sara's hand and they closed their eyes like they had as girls and released their wishes into the universe. "What did you wish for?" Julia asked.

"I'm not falling for that one again," Sara said. "I want it to come true."

They laughed at the interplay between past and present, and then watched the stars a little longer. The half-moon cast a dim light over the courtyard.

"I feel better now," Sara said. "We can go back inside if you want."

"Are you sure?" Julia said.

"I'm sure," Sara said. "Now I have a more pressing problem." She picked up her scarf and tied it around her shoulders.

"What?" Julia asked.

"I'm in serious danger of sobering up," Sara said.

"That *is* serious," Julia laughed.

Sara apologized to Max and Melanie when they returned to the living room. "I have my own built-in fireplace, these days."

"Happens to the best of us," Melanie said.

Max's brow momentarily furrowed. "I feel oddly left out of this conversation," he said.

"I hear there's such a thing as male menopause, too," Julia said. "The symptoms just show up in different ways. Like red Ferraris, and younger women. It's still heat. Just acted *out* instead of in."

Melanie applauded Julia's insight.

"I can't imagine what you mean," Max said, his innocence perfected.

"Bullshit, darling," Melanie said. She placed another small log on the fire.

"Yes, bullshit, Max," Julia agreed.

"Well, I know when it's time for me to leave a room," Max said jovially. "You girls can talk about ovaries and whatever else for as long as you want. I think I'll turn in."

"I'll join you," Melanie said. "I have a sexy little red number I might try on for you."

"I need to put away the Ferrari first," Max smiled.

They said their goodnights and left Julia and Sara sitting across from each other in the expansive living room. Sara poured another glass of wine and Julia motioned for her to sit closer. Sara joined her on the sofa. The room was quiet except for the intermittent hiss and crackle of the fire.

"Feeling better?" Julia asked.

"Actually, I'm starting to feel quite good," she said. "But I'm not sure if it's because of the surroundings or the wine."

"Maybe a little of both," Julia said.

The events of Sara's day began to fade, becoming dreamlike. Had she really considered sleeping with the young waiter from the café? Perhaps she had also imagined her feelings for Julia the day before.

"I'm sorry I didn't stay in touch after you left," Sara said. "You sent all these post cards and letters that I never answered."

"I have to admit that was hard," Julia said. "We had been such good friends. And then you just disappeared."

"I felt so abandoned," Sara said truthfully.

Julia rested her hand on Sara's. "I've really missed you. I didn't realize how much until you got here."

"I've missed you, too," Sara said.

Julia's words repeated in her mind. It was nice to be missed. Especially by Julia. This brought more pleasure to her than she wanted to admit. "Can I tell you something else?" Sara asked.

"Of course, anything."

"Even if it sounds crazy?"

"Especially if it sounds crazy. I love crazy. The crazier the better." Julia smiled.

"Despite the hot flashes and momentary lapses of terror, I haven't felt this good in a really long time. It's not normal for me to feel this good."

"I hate to think of you being so unhappy," Julia said.

"Maybe I'm just being overly dramatic," Sara said. "After all, I am a drama and English teacher at Beacon High."

"Remember Mrs. McGregor?" Julia asked. "She could have definitely used Botox."

They looked at each other and laughed.

"We were really awful back then, weren't we?" Sara said.

"Not any worse than everybody else," Julia said.

Somehow it didn't matter how silly they were being, or that they were grown, supposedly sophisticated, women. "I've always loved your laugh," Julia said.

Sara leaned into Julia's shoulder feeling the sweet warmth of Julia's company and the wine. The look on Julia's face had so much love in it, it caught Sara by surprise. Was this what happiness was? To have someone look at you with that much love and acceptance?

The small fire crackled loudly. Sara finished the last sip of her wine and stared into the empty glass. A single tear trailed down her cheek and dropped into the folds of her scarf. Her next thought surprised her. She suddenly didn't want to die. She wanted another chance at life; a chance to celebrate it instead of simply endure it. She had wasted so many years living a pseudo-life and taking things for granted. Not realizing what a privilege it was to flounder around and make mistakes and participate in this giant experiment of humanity.

Julia laced her fingers in Sara's. Her hand felt to Sara like a rope thrown down into a deep well that she must grab onto to save her life.

Sara observed their interlocking fingers and couldn't tell where Julia's hand ended and hers began. She wanted to absorb Julia's confidence in a palm to palm transfusion.

"I wish you'd tell me what's going on," Julia said.

When Julia squeezed Sara's hand again, a charge of desire moved through her body like an electrical current. Sara jerked away as if she had been shocked.

"What is it?" Julia asked.

"Nothing," Sara said.

"It sure doesn't seem like nothing," Julia said.

Sara pulled her knees to her chest and retied the scarf around her neck as if to retie her composure. Her mind raced to explain the feeling away. She thought of those Middle Eastern countries where the men veiled their women in an effort to avoid temptation. Sara wished Julia were veiled now. Yet avoiding the temptation seemed hardly the cure. If anything, it served more to ignite it.

Julia's face was radiant in the soft light and full of questions. "Sara, what is it?"

"Do you mind if we go outside?" Sara asked. She suddenly couldn't breathe. Sara left the living room and passed through the double doors to the courtyard. She followed the runway of lights that outlined the walkway. The red scarf fell loosely around her shoulders. Moonlight reflected in the water at the Lady's feet. Her open arms threatened Sara now. She was too open, too accepting.

Sara retreated to the bench in front of the fountain. The moonlight lit up the virgin's face. Julia had followed and joined her on the bench. She touched Sara's knee. Heat raised the length of Sara's body. It wasn't a hot flash, although she wished it were. Sara wanted a biological reason for what she was feeling. Or any reason that might circumvent the truth.

"This is wrong," Sara said.

"What is?" Julia asked, as if genuinely confused.

"I'm married to Grady," she said, more to herself than to Julia. "I have children. I'm a Republican, for God's sake."

Julia laughed. "Well, I guess technically, I am, too. But what does that have to do with anything?"

Sara dissolved deeper into her confusion. Not even her politics had been something she had chosen out of clear conviction. She was a Republican because Grady was. Basically, she had voted for whoever Grady told her to.

"Sara, what's going on?" Julia reached her hand toward Sara's, but Sara refused it. The wine's effect had faded.

"Julia, there's something I need to tell you." She wondered herself what it was she was about to confess. The cancer? Or the more urgent one of desire.

Julia's face turned serious. "What is it, honey?"

Sara paused. "I have cancer."

When she saw the pain on Julia's face she wished she had chosen the other confession. "Cancer?" Julia asked.

"It's okay, I'm in remission." Sara lied so the look would go away. She didn't want to cause Julia any pain.

"When did you find out?" Julia asked.

Sara filled her in on the events of the last year, as well as her problems with Grady, and her sudden decision to take a sabbatical and come to Italy. She left out the part about her cancer coming back and the uncertainty of her future. Somehow it felt like she had already shared too much.

Julia was quiet for a long time as she took it all in. "I can't imagine what this is like for you," she said.

"It hasn't been easy," Sara said. "But in a way I'm grateful for it. You know, I've never felt as alive as I have on this trip. And I can't afford to fool myself anymore. Life gets really simple when you think you might die."

Julia took Sara's hand again and this time she didn't resist it. "I think you must be the bravest person I've ever known. I'm so glad you decided to come to Italy."

Sara laughed. "That's a new one. How can someone as cowardly as me be brave?"

"Well you are." Julia leaned in and kissed Sara on the cheek.

The imprint of Julia's lips felt hot on Sara's face. Sara leaned toward Julia to return the kiss on the cheek but instead kissed her on the lips. Julia's mouth opened slightly and their tongues touched, exploring the intimate new territory of each other's mouths for a moment.

Sara's body began to tremble. She waited for the ground to yawn open and swallow her. At the very least she expected Julia's reaction to be one of disgust or disapproval. Instead, Julia's face revealed only a glimmer of surprise.

Within seconds, Sara's momentary bravery retreated, leaving her feeling raw and exposed. She was someone who exercised, ate right, and still got cancer. Someone who had kept a safe distance and still fell in love with her best friend.

Julia called out her name as Sara ran out of the garden.

Chapter Thirteen

What have I done? Sara thought.

Coming to Italy had shattered her perceptions of herself. She was someone totally different than she had always thought. The cancer had eradicated the rules and restrictions she had held herself to for all these years. She had kissed Julia. She had kissed her best friend. How could this possibly be a good thing?

Sara grabbed a set of car keys hanging on the hook by the kitchen door.

"Where are you going?" Julia caught up with her.

"I need to get out of here," Sara said. "I need to find an airport and fly home." Julia followed her through the courtyard to the driveway. Sara slid into the driver's side of Max's small BMW. Julia jumped into the passenger side.

"Sara, let's talk about this," Julia said. She turned to face her. "Try to stay calm. There's nowhere to go tonight," she continued. "We can leave in the morning if you want."

"I need to go home *now!*" Sara's voice had a desperation to it that she had never heard before. She fumbled with the car keys and started the motor of Max's car. Sara jerked the gears into first and splayed gravel behind the car. "This is crazy," Julia yelled, hanging onto the dashboard. "Stop this car this instant!"

Sara stopped. They jerked forward. "Are you trying to kill us?" Julia's voice reached for calmness, but didn't quite make it.

"Get out of the car," Sara ordered Julia.

Julia didn't move.

Sara accelerated down the long driveway made of dirt mixed with gravel. The headlights illuminated a small rectangle of the countryside in front of them. She was reminded of her drive out into the New England countryside months before.

Julia hurriedly fastened her seat belt. Sara left hers off.

If she flew through the windshield on impact, so much the better, she thought.

Life had taken an unexpected turn and she had no idea how to deal with it. She was a stranger to herself. A random thought confirmed that she actually liked this stranger, much more than the old Sara. But it was too late for thoughts like that. She accelerated down the long driveway.

"Where are you going?" Julia asked.

"I have no idea," Sara said truthfully, "but you're free to get out at any time."

"Stop this!" Julia insisted. She placed her hand on Sara's arm.

The touch was enough to pull Sara's glance in Julia's direction. Julia's eyes were wide and alarmed. Sara was scaring her. She hated this thought. But what she hated more, at that moment, was herself. She knew she was acting crazy but she couldn't seem to stop herself. Sara slammed on the brakes again. The car skidded. The earthy smell of dirt rose from its sleep and filled the car. Sara glared at Julia, challenging her to let her go, to let her drive out into the night to rejoin her old, safe life.

"Be reasonable," Julia said.

"Is that the best you can come up with?" Sara asked. "You sound like Grady. *Be reasonable,* Sara. *Don't make waves,* Sara."

Julia didn't back down from Sara's gaze. In that instant Sara recognized the lawyer part of Julia, that was trained to act calm and in control of the situation.

Sara put the car in gear again, this time accelerating much slower. They passed a grove of olive trees. For the second time in her life she contemplated running into the middle of the trees, sacrificing herself against their twisted trunks. But she would never hurt Julia. Never. She reached the end of the driveway and stopped. There were no signposts either way.

"I don't know what to do," Sara said, white-knuckling the steering wheel.

"That's okay," Julia said softly. "We'll figure it out together."

Sara lowered her head onto her hands on the steering wheel and quietly began to sob.

Chapter Fourteen

The next morning Julia knocked softly on the door of the guest room. "Can we talk for a minute?" she said from behind the door.

Sara reached up and touched where her lips had met Julia's the night before. She traced a path in her mind she had never explored. Her temples throbbed; she felt hung-over. She had not slept. She had played the scene from the night before over and over in her mind. Had she really taken Julia hostage in the car and driven like a maniac into the night?

Julia knocked again. Sara walked to the door, grateful for its solid barrier. But Julia's tangible presence on the other side felt like heat radiating from a sidewalk. "What do you want?" Sara asked. She rested her cheek against the wood.

"We need to talk," Julia said, her voice muffled.

"I don't know if I can," Sara sighed. "Besides, haven't you had enough of me?"

"Let's talk," Julia repeated.

Sara paused, the checks and balances of a lifetime being weighed. She slowly opened the door and stepped aside, leaving Julia room to enter. Once she was inside, Sara closed the door behind her.

Julia sat on the bed. Sara wrapped her bathrobe close against her chest and avoided looking directly at her. "I'm so sorry," Sara said, with renewed humility. "I don't know what came over me. I don't usually kiss women or take my friends hostage for wild midnight rides."

"That's why we need to talk," Julia said. "About the kiss. You need to know you didn't do anything wrong."

Sara laughed. "A great many people would disagree with you, Julia."

"You sound like you may be one of those people."

"Maybe I am."

Julia paused, as if thinking through an argument for a case. "There are people who judge whatever they don't understand," Julia said. "But this isn't about them, it's about us."

"But I kissed you." Sara threw these words across the room, like fuel on a flame to make her shame burn brighter. She lowered her voice, "I'm not a lesbian."

"I'm not, either," Julia said. "I think labels are useless in this instance, anyway. But it was real. It was honest. Friends kiss each other all the time."

"Not like that!" Sara countered, a crimson reminder crossing her face.

"No, not like that," Julia agreed. "But it wasn't awful in the least, Sara. It was just different. And strange for both of us, I suppose, because we've never kissed each other before."

Sara touched her lips and quickly withdrew her hand. "I'm sorry for the dramatics last night," she said. "Do you hate me?"

"Of course I don't hate you. Quite the contrary."

Sara walked to the window overlooking the courtyard and the stone icon. For several seconds she was quiet. "I wonder what she would say about all this," Sara said, motioning to the statue in the garden.

"Honestly, I don't think she would mind," Julia said. "Deities are very understanding from what I hear."

Sara stood at the window for several more seconds before joining Julia on the bed. She hung onto the bedpost as though it was a life raft bobbing around in a deep sea. A brief laugh rode on a wave of regret. She hadn't even told Julia about the young waiter at the café. What was going on with her? At her age, did she suddenly have a libido? Or was it that she needed to prove to herself that she was still alive?

"You're not losing it," Julia said, as if she had heard Sara's thoughts. "You kissed me. Big deal. And if I were totally honest I'd have to say I rather enjoyed it."

"You enjoyed it?"

"Yes, I did," Julia said. "I've never kissed a woman before. Not that the possibility hasn't entered my mind from time to time. But I have to admit it felt perfectly natural."

Their eyes met. Was Julia telling the truth? "I liked kissing you, too," Sara said finally. She lowered her head, as though this confession carried with it the penitence of a hundred Hail Mary's. "What do we do now?"

Sara wanted Julia to take the lead, like she had countless times when they were girls. She wanted Julia to tell her that she didn't see her that way, that the kiss was nice, but a one-time thing. Case closed. Years from now they would laugh about that crazy night in Siena, a product of too much wine and too much Italy.

"It's an interesting situation," Julia said. "But whatever happens, I think we can handle it. Our friendship has endured this long, right? I think it's destined to survive, no matter what."

"I like thinking about our friendship that way," Sara said.

"Just promise me, no more driving off into the night, okay?" And please don't torment yourself. Life is too short." Julia stopped herself, as if she realized what she had said.

Sara extended her hand across the bed and created a bridge between them. "Life *is* too short," she said.

"What's going on with you two?" Max asked over breakfast later that morning.

"Yes, you're both awfully quiet," Melanie said, as if her interest had suddenly been aroused.

"Quiet?" Julia asked. She took a sip of fresh-squeezed orange juice and glanced in Sara's direction.

"We stayed up late talking," Sara said, "I guess we're just tired."

Sara trusted Julia would not talk about last night. Yet what had happened between them night before seemed to be the uninvited guest to their breakfast table. The looks between them had changed. It was as if their friendship would now be divided into two clear time distinctions: before and after the kiss. But even that revelation was not the most significant to Sara. Although she had suffered mortification on many levels, Sara found herself wanting to kiss Julia again. Was this what being alive was about? One temptation after another? Sara bolted down the espresso in front of her, wishing for something stronger. All her needs had woken up at once.

"We thought we might go into Siena today, if we can borrow the car," Julia said.

"Of course," Max said.

Sara glanced in Julia's direction. They hadn't talked about any plans for the day. But perhaps an adventure in Siena would take her mind off of everything and return her to her usual state of pleasantly numb.

"I'll cook tonight," Julia said. "If Max doesn't mind sharing his kitchen."

"Not at all. In fact, that would be fabulous." Max folded his newspaper and placed it on the table. "You're in for a real treat, Sara. Julia's the best."

A piece of Italian pastry lodged in Sara's throat. A fit of coughing followed. Her audience watched, as if trying to decide whether to laugh or perform the Heimlich maneuver. The obstruction cleared. Sara reassured everyone that she was fine.

Throughout their day in Siena, Sara caught Julia studying her like a riddle whose complexity had challenged her to the point of distraction. Sara's defenses, in the recent past, had been as solid as Siena's city walls. But now it appeared that the walls were crumbling. The beauty of this ancient city was weakening her.

It hardly mattered that Sara had just been there the day before. Siena was breathtaking. They entered a street Sara recognized.

"There's a lovely café just around the corner," Julia said. "Why don't we go there for lunch?"

Sara realized it was Antonio's café and she tried to come up with an excuse why this wouldn't work. But before she came up with anything Julia had pulled her inside. A small bell announced their entry. Sara quickly scanned the café for Antonio and exhaled her relief when he was nowhere in sight.

They sat at a table and an older man greeted them. He looked like an older version of Antonio. He recognized Julia and smiled widely at her, saying something in Italian. Julia answered him in Italian and ordered two cappuccinos.

"You should see his son," Julia arched her eyebrows.

"His son?"

"Is there something wrong?" Julia asked. "You look practically ashen."

"I'm fine," Sara said. "I'm just sorry I don't get the meet the son." *Relieved*, she wanted to say.

"But you do," Julia said, motioning toward the back. "He's bringing our order."

Sara clutched her purse in her lap to anchor herself and keep from running out the door. Antonio smiled when he recognized her and Sara lowered her eyes. He placed the cappuccinos on their table and then left.

"He's gorgeous, isn't he?" Julia asked.

Sara nodded and sipped her cappuccino too soon, burning her lips.

"Doesn't he bear a slight resemblance to Michelangelo's David?" Julia asked.

That was the same thing Sara had thought, but she didn't share this with Julia.

"But he's not that great in bed," Julia added in a whisper.

A slight gasp escaped from Sara's lips.

"Did I shock you, Sweetie?" Julia looked pleased.

"No, not at all," Sara said, which wasn't true. It was indeed shocking to hear that Julia had also been in the young waiter's apartment and had actually tried out the bed. Her life had become a soap opera episode.

This kind of thing doesn't happen to me, Sara thought.

She missed the saucer when returning her cup to the table and spilled her entire drink. Sara threw a napkin on her mistake and to keep it from spilling in her lap.

"I can't believe this," Sara mumbled.

Antonio returned with a rag to clean up the mess. His attention stayed focused on Sara, a fact that was not lost on Julia. Antonio offered Sara a brief, radiant smile before walking away.

"Do you know him?" Julia asked.

"A little bit," Sara said. "Yesterday when you had to go to Florence I ended up here. Funny coincidence, isn't it?"

Sara noted a slight smile on Julia's face. "Sara, did you go out with him, too?" She seemed to take pleasure in this possibility.

"Well, we may have gotten together for a little while."

"You got together?"

Sara was enjoying the look of surprise on Julia's face. "He wanted to show me a part of Siena I'd never seen before."

"And did he?"

Sara wondered briefly if Julia was simply curious, or a bit jealous.

"If you mean his small fourth floor apartment, where dirty dishes were stacked to the ceiling and his smelly clothes lined the floor? Then, yes."

Julia laughed. "Sara, I'm genuinely shocked. All this time I thought you were Demeter and it turns out you are Aphrodite."

Sara knew enough about mythology to take this as a complement. Demeter was a mother goddess who took care of everyone. Aphrodite was sensual and seductive, the goddess of love.

"Did you?" Julia asked.

"Sleep with him?"

Julia nodded.

"No, I backed out at the last minute."

Sara studied the young man from across the café. Was he Julia's type, this young, athletic Adonis? Was he hers? Whose type wouldn't he be? was the better question.

"So will you see him again?" Julia asked.

"I'd be more inclined to clean up his apartment," Sara said.

Julia laughed. "You never cease to amaze me," she said.

"Sometimes I amaze myself," Sara said. She leaned in and whispered. "So he wasn't that good in bed?" Now it was her turn to wonder if she was asking this out of curiosity or jealousy.

"The packaging is much better than the delivery," Julia said. "Surely you've known men like that."

"Well, not really," Sara said. "Grady's the only man I've ever slept with."

Julia looked surprised again. "You poor, sweet girl," she said. She rested her hand on Sara's for several seconds. Sara's palm began to sweat.

Antonio returned to ask if they needed anything. Sara had to resist looking at his packaging. She was relieved now that she hadn't slept with him.

After he left, Julia smiled and leaned toward her. "He seems captivated with you."

But Sara didn't care. As the day progressed she was becoming more and more captivated with Julia. Antonio offered little or no attraction. She and Julia had a history together and the intimacy earned by a long friendship. Not to mention that the kiss had been the most amazing she had ever experienced. "Can we go?" Sara asked.

Julia nodded. They left the café and walked along the streets of Siena and temporarily mingled with a flock of tourists being led by a tour guide speaking German. The tour guide was an exceedingly tall woman who wore a bright yellow blouse. She carried a car antenna with a yellow feather dangling from the top to keep her flock together.

"Tweedy-Bird meets Brünhilde." Sara motioned in the woman's direction.

Julia laughed and locked her arm in Sara's, something she had done often when they had walked the streets of Florence. But this time Sara's body stiffened. Her attraction felt like a potential wildfire fanning out in search of something to ignite.

At least she wasn't bored with her life anymore. If anything, it had become too exciting. In a matter of days, she had the makings of a memoir.

Later that evening Julia and Sara had the kitchen to themselves. Sara had, more or less successfully, spent the day pretending that nothing out of the ordinary had happened the night before. Yet all she could think about was how beautiful Julia was.

Julia tied a red apron around her waist as Sara sat on a nearby stool. Something about the apron felt familiar. Soft music played in the background, a collection of Bach cello sonatas. Julia arranged her workspace and collected the ingredients she would need, dividing her focus between Sara and the cooking preparations.

"I don't usually have an audience," she said, "except for Roberto and Bella."

"Would you like me to leave?" Sara asked, hoping the answer would be no.

"Stay and keep me company," Julia said. "But I need to know why you're staring at me."

"It's your apron," Sara said. "I just remembered a dream I had last night. You were wearing a red apron almost exactly like the one you're wearing now."

"Isn't it interesting that we're having dreams of each other?" Julia asked. "What do you think the dream means?"

"Who knows," Sara said. "Maybe it's a premonition. Or maybe it's confirmation that I'm supposed to be here right now. Like it's destiny."

"I'd like to think our being together has something to do with destiny." Julia chopped and minced a garlic clove and its pungent aroma escaped into the kitchen.

"I hadn't given destiny much thought until a year or so ago," Sara said.

"Because of the cancer?"

"Yes," Sara said. "It makes you think about all sorts of things."

Julia wiped her hands on her apron. "I'm so glad you've got that all behind you," Julia smiled. She sliced a green pepper with swift, easy strokes on a nearby cutting board. "You don't know how nice it is to be with someone who can talk about serious things," she added.

"I feel the same way," Sara said.

Julia continued her preparations and then set them aside. She took a sip of wine. "Are you still upset about last night?"

"I've been trying not to think about it," Sara said. "I'm hoping that it can be our secret forever."

"I'm good at secrets," Julia said.

"You always were." Sara paused, wondering what had happened to the guilt and remorse from the night before. For some reason she felt perfectly calm.

"You know, Sara, I think Italy suits you. You look practically radiant." Julia held up her wine glass and saluted her.

Sara wondered if it was Italy that suited her or Julia.

Julia prepared strawberries, pears and kiwi for a fruit salad. In the process she walked over and placed a strawberry in Sara's mouth. The gesture seemed innocent on Julia's part but to Sara it was deeply sensuous. The wine continued to loosen Sara's reserve. She savored the fruit and the desire to kiss Julia again, a desire she had swallowed most of the day. And a desire, thanks to the wine, that was asserting itself with renewed bravado.

Julia dropped a handful of pasta into the boiling water. Even cooking pasta felt sexy in Sara's current mood. She finished the red wine in her glass. Something about it tasted earthy, sensuous, as if an act of communing with the body and blood of Tuscany.

Sara thought back over the last couple of days. There had been more than one surprise. Several, in fact. She thought again of how she had called this her farewell tour. So why not do a few things she might regret? What did she have to lose?

"I feel like I'm standing on the edge of a high dive and trying to decide whether to jump," Sara said.

Julia turned to face her. "It must look pretty scary from there," she said, as if she understood.

"But what if I don't know how to swim? What if my heart just can't take it?"

This kind of 'what if' talking always irritated Grady. It was too abstract. But Julia nodded thoughtfully and walked around the island in the kitchen to stand next to Sara who was still sitting on the stool. Julia caressed Sara's cheek. Her touch was soft, loving.

"There's something I've wanted to do all day," Julia said. She lifted Sara's chin and leaned in to kiss her.

The kitchen door burst open. "How's it going in here?" Melanie asked.

Their brief connection ended, a switch thrown, instantly separating them from its power source.

"Your timing is impeccable," Julia smiled.

Melanie covered her eyes and apologized. She turned and left the room, a slight smile on her face, as the door fanned her heels.

"I don't think I've ever seen Melanie so embarrassed," Julia said.

"I know how she feels," Sara said. "I wonder how long it will take her to tell Max."

"Maybe a millisecond," Julia laughed.

Sara squeezed her temples, anticipating the headache that would come. Within seconds the old Sara had returned. The Sara that played by the rules imposed by society. "I'm sorry, Julia. I seem to be playing with fire these days. We need to stop this. We need to stop this now."

"Do we?" Julia asked. "I've been thinking about that, and I'm not so sure."

In another week Sara would be going home to her safe, predictable life. Meanwhile, she was in a foreign land, experiencing foreign desires. At that moment, she had no idea what she wanted. Or did she?

Julia's acceptance was like an aphrodisiac. If not for the crowd of dreaded Puritans looking up from the bottom of her gene pool, she might have taken the plunge with Julia already.

Chapter Fifteen

It was Sara's last morning at Max and Melanie's before returning to Florence. She rose and opened the wooden shutters to view the courtyard. The lady of the fountain stood in the early morning sun, her stone gown still in shadow. She looked eternal, like the sunrise. Julia knocked on the door and Sara let her in.

"I heard you open your shutters," Julia said. "How's your headache?"

Sara had retired early the night before blaming a non-existent migraine. The truth was she had lost her courage. Being with Julia challenged not only sociological barriers, but emotional ones, as well. This was actually someone who she could fall in love with and someone who could break her heart.

They stood at the window looking down into the courtyard at the statue. "I don't want to leave her," Sara said. "This sounds crazy but it feels like she's one of the reasons I came. Not in a religious sense. But something bigger. Like I'm here to get some kind of archetypal acceptance."

"I forget sometimes how much goes on underneath that quiet persona of yours," Julia said, not taking her eyes from the courtyard.

"Thanks for not laughing at me," Sara said.

Julia leaned into Sara's shoulder. "I wouldn't dream of it."

For the next several seconds Sara attempted to memorize the scene before her: the courtyard, the Tuscan countryside, and Julia at her side. To say that she didn't want the moment to end was a cliché. But it was true. Sara wanted to reset the timer on her life and begin a new lifetime right there. She would have no regrets for the first half of her life. It had served its purpose. Now, the second half would be lived with intention.

That is, if I'm granted a second half, she thought.

Later that morning Max and Melanie drove Julia and Sara to the train station. A slight melancholy rode along with Sara as she viewed the Tuscan countryside, its rolling hills, sans trees, except for the occasional olive grove and trees planted around a farmhouse here and there.

"It's been incredible," she said to Max and Melanie. "I can't tell you how much it's meant to me to be here."

Max and Melanie had been totally accepting of the events in the kitchen the night before and Sara had to resist telling them that nothing had actually happened. At least not physically.

"Please come to visit at any time," Melanie said.

"I may take you up on that," Sara said.

"I hope you do," Max said.

They embraced. Max and Melanie felt like old friends even after a weekend together, and Sara hated to think that she might never see them again.

"Are you all right?" Julia asked her, once they had settled on the train. "You've been very quiet all morning."

"I guess I've just been deep in thought," Sara said. Her Italian vacation was halfway over and this fact made her melancholy deeper.

"Anything you want to talk about?" Julia asked. She reached over and touched Sara's hand and then removed it.

Julia had not forced anything between them. Sara realized now that this would have been the only way that anything between them would have ever worked. Otherwise, Sara might have blamed Julia for coercing her, for creating the raging current in which she had gotten swept away.

The train began to pull out of the small station in Siena. It seemed too simple for the town it serviced. Sara stared out the window, as she always did on trains. She hadn't realized until this trip how much she loved trains. They made her feel hopeful. It meant a journey was underway. A journey where she could actually see and experience the distance she traveled unlike the abstract miles of a plane.

A woman leaned out a second-story window watching the train with a wistful look. Sara recognized the expression on the woman's face as one she had experienced herself. The woman appeared slightly younger than Sara, with long brown hair and a white loose blouse. Sara was close enough to see three silver bracelets on her left arm.

For a few seconds their eyes met. The look they exchanged held an entire conversation within it. With this glance, Sara knew that the woman wanted to be on the train, too. She wanted to be going somewhere. But something stopped her.

Sara told her, in this silent conversation, that she understood. She told her not to lose hope. She told her that if Sara could get to Italy, the woman could get to anywhere she wanted, too.

It's never too late to get what you want, Sara wanted to tell her.

As the train passed Sara placed her fingers on the glass. The woman gave Sara a brief wave. Had she heard their unspoken conversation?

Sara's sadness turned to gratitude. The woman had given her a gift: a snapshot of herself just a few weeks before. Everything had changed since then. She now believed in impossible things. And she also now believed that life, when left to its own devices, had a much bigger imagination than Sara had. The last thing Sara would have predicted of her trip to Italy was that she would fall in love with Julia.

The absolute last thing, she thought.

But she now believed that this was what had happened. And she wondered if she hadn't always been a little in love with Julia.

"You know, Jules, I'm tired of being so afraid," Sara said, as she continued to stare out the window.

"What makes you say that?"

The train accelerated until the Italian countryside streamed by as rapidly as Sara's thoughts. She practiced the words in her head before speaking them.

"I want to be with you, Julia."

Her right leg began to shake and she steadied it. Sara didn't know how Julia would respond, but she trusted her to be kind.

Julia placed her hand on Sara's. "I want to be with you, too," she said softly.

Chapter Sixteen

Roberto parted the blue sea of the quilt between them and made his way to the head of the bed. Sara rubbed his whiskers and face and he leaned into her hand. He had been very affectionate with Sara since she and Julia had returned from Siena. Bella was much more reserved with her affection. No longer able to sleep on her usual pillow next to Julia, she took up residence on the sofa in the living room where Sara had slept the first few days of her visit.

The last three days had been, in a word, unbelievable. Sara had never spent so much time horizontal. Their initial awkwardness with each other's bodies had disappeared. Aphrodite had indeed come alive in her. It was as if she had fallen in love with love.

At the beginning of this journey she had found herself within the pages of a self-help book and at a crossroads. Now she was living within a Shakespeare love sonnet. And despite her realization of how unrealistic and out of control this was feeling, she never wanted to leave.

Sara waited for Julia to wake up and wondered briefly if Grady had remembered to walk Luke. He had little patience with animals and Luke liked to take his time on his morning walks. Sara pushed this thought away, along with the awareness that she would be leaving Italy in four days.

Roberto walked delicately across Julia's pillow. She reached up to pet him.

"*Buon giorno*, Roberto," she said sleepily.

Julia often spoke to him in Italian. Her reasoning being, as she had told Sara a few days before, that Roberto was from a litter down the street so of course he only understood Italian.

Julia glanced up at Sara with one eye open and smiled. Sara pushed Julia's hair out of her hazel eyes and was struck again by how quickly life could change. Not only was it unbelievable that Sara was in Italy, but also that she had taken up residence in Julia's bed.

Sara ran her hand along the curve of Julia's hip. It was as if Sara's hand belonged to someone else. Someone in love with the female form. She had never particularly liked her own body. But she was learning a new appreciation for it. In the last forty-eight hours she had surprised herself almost continuously. Not only with the tenderness that she extended toward Julia but also by the amount of passion that had been present in their lovemaking.

"*Buon giorno*, darling," Julia said softly to Sara.

They kissed, as Roberto rode the waves of arms and elbows caused by the wake of their embrace. Under the covers they blended together, skin against skin. Sara loved the sensuousness of this. Of becoming one with someone. Not knowing where Julia ended and where she began.

Julia ran her finger along the scar on Sara's chest and kissed it. "It's ugly, isn't it?" Sara said.

"Not at all," Julia said. She leaned on one arm and looked in Sara's eyes. "If not for this scar, you might not be here at all."

Pressure rose from beneath the scar, as if Sara's heart insisted on expanding. These were new feelings to her, and at times, overwhelming feelings. Could someone die from too much happiness?

Sara sat up and leaned against the back of Julia's bed. She was reminded again of her farewell tour.

"Shall we go out today?" Sara said. "We've hardly left your apartment since we returned from Siena."

Julia smiled and sat up, as well. "If we must."

"Your neighbors may be wondering if you're all right," Sara said.

"They're used to me disappearing periodically. Especially when I get inspired."

"Are you inspired now?"

"Definitely," Julia said. She leaned over and pulled Sara closer. They kissed and Julia pulled her gently down on the bed.

"Wait a minute, honey," Sara said. At that moment, their closeness felt dangerous. As if Sara had suddenly become conscious of the air she needed to breathe. She was disarmed and vulnerable to Julia's slightest wish. Did Julia feel vulnerable, too? She got up from the bed and her knees momentarily weakened.

"I need fresh air," Sara said. She put on her light housecoat and walked out onto the balcony.

The early morning sun bounced from building to building through the alley way and danced on the top of the tree in the courtyard below.

I could spend the rest of my life here, Sara thought, and then erased the thought from her mind.

By early afternoon they were dressed and in front of Julia's building. "Where shall we go?" Julia asked.

"You decide," Sara said. She squinted at the brightness of the sun, longing briefly to return to Julia's darkened bedroom. It felt good to take a break from their intensity. Being in Italy felt like a dream. Especially now that she was in love. She had never even approached that level of happiness except briefly at the birth of each of her children. Even Sam, her unplanned child, had brought her unexpected joy by his arrival.

What would her children think of this new version of Sara? Would they be happy for her? Would they celebrate her happiness? Sara was afraid to test them on this point.

They walked several blocks passing buildings with heavy ornate wooden doors, barricades, Julia told her, against enemy intruder's centuries before. The Arno River meandered through the heart of the city. They crossed a bridge and waited at a traffic light while a parade of small children on bicycles and tricycles passed by; their parents following close behind, pushing strollers carrying younger siblings.

"It's nice to see that such an ancient city could embrace so many children," Sara said.

"The things that go through your mind," Julia said.

"Am I boring you?"

"Absolutely not," Julia said.

They paused to let the procession pass. "I can't imagine what it's like to live here and see this beauty every day," Sara said. "Do you get numb to it?"

"I haven't yet," Julia said. "But the most beautiful sight right now is you."

"I am resisting kissing you right now," Sara said as they waited on the last section of the parade. "It hardly seems fair that we have to hide our love for each other," she added. "The world could use more love."

"We don't have to hide it," Julia said.

"Yes we do," Sara said and warned her with her eyes. Did she fear the world's judgment or her own?

Julia took Sara's hand, pulling her across the now clear street and away from her thoughts. "Are you hungry?" she asked.

"Starving," Sara replied.

Not only for food, she thought, *but also for Julia.*

Who was this person she had become? It wasn't like her to be insatiable about anything, especially life.

They entered a restaurant down a quiet street. A dark, intimate oasis with only one other couple inside having a late lunch. Sara ordered, using the little bit of Italian she had picked up on her trip and Julia applauded her attempt.

The waiter brought them a small bottle of wine and poured them each a glass. Julia watched Sara, as she had so often on her visit. "What are you thinking about?" Sara said, after the waiter left.

"I was thinking that it's been an amazing couple of days," Julia said.

Sara lowered her eyes. "I have to admit, I didn't see this one coming. Do you suppose we're having some kind of mid-life crisis?"

"Well if we are, I hope it lasts for a long time," Julia smiled. She reached over and held Sara's hand and Sara automatically looked around to make sure no one was looking. "Relax, darling. No one cares," she added.

"I can't seem to get past the stigma of it," Sara said.

"Stigma?" Julia asked.

"You're reducing what we have to a stigma?"

Sara apologized. She knew she was being unreasonable. But wasn't the world being unreasonable, too?

Later that afternoon they strolled the narrow streets, ducking into an occasional shop. Julia spoke to everyone as if she knew them. They stopped and ate gelato at Julia's favorite shop, and Sara remembered their days of banana Popsicles and long summer afternoons where their friendship basked in the sun by the Connecticut River. Then they found a shady bench in a park nearby and began to excavate the frozen delicacy from the white scalloped plastic cup.

"How do you tell the tourists from the locals?" Sara asked.

"The athletic shoes always give the Americans away." Julia gestured toward a rotund man in front of them wearing blue spandex shorts, striped socks, and sneakers the exact shade of blue as his shorts. "That took some planning," she added.

Sara nudged Julia's arm and looked down at her sandals, relieved that she might be mistaken for a local. Minutes passed. A juggler began a performance in the distance. A cool breeze blew through the trees. "I could stay here forever," Sara said, voicing her thought from earlier that day.

"Feel free," Julia said.

Sara laughed. "A remote possibility, at best."

"I'm serious," Julia said.

Pigeons searched for crumbs at their feet. "Let's not talk about this now," Sara said. As she stood, the pigeons scattered. She walked in the direction they had come, over stepping stones of sunlight beaming through the trees. She wanted to run but walked briskly instead. The juggler winked at her as she walked past, his rhythm undisturbed. Julia caught up with her.

"Are you angry?" she asked.

"No, it's just that you say things like that as if it's easy."

"Isn't it?" Julia asked.

"Of course not," Sara said. "Listen, I don't want to talk about it right now. Let's just enjoy our day, okay?"

Sara locked her arm in Julia's. Their sunny day had a cloud on the horizon. For the first time ever, she was the one to lead Julia home.

Chapter Seventeen

The Sunday *New York Times* was spread out on the bed in front of them. Sara skimmed the latest stories about their unpopular president who at Grady's suggestion she had voted for twice. Life in the States had continued on without her. In two days she would be leaving. This felt as tragic as all the stories on the front page combined. Sara sighed and sat up in bed.

"What is it?" Julia asked.

"We need to talk." Sara sounded as serious as she felt.

"I have a better idea." Julia kissed Sara's neck.

"Honey, stop," Sara said, intent on injecting them with a potent shot of reality. She was too old to fall this completely for someone. She was acting like a teenager again. Or maybe a teenager for the first time. Nothing like this had ever happened to her. This was the first time love had actually ever felt like an act of falling. In this case, a freefall from an airplane without a parachute. She and Grady hadn't fallen in love. They had fallen in comfort with one another.

Julia turned serious and sat up and stacked her pillows behind her. "Okay, let's talk," she said.

Sara forced herself not to look at Julia or she might lose her courage. She cleared her throat, as if the seriousness of what she was about to say required the utmost of vocal clarity. "I've fallen in love with you," Sara announced. Her confession sounded stiff and unconvincing, even to her.

"I've fallen in love with you, too." Julia's expression matched Sara's seriousness. Was she anticipating what was coming next?

"But you're my best friend," Sara said.

"Don't we all fall in love with our best friends?" Julia asked. "Maybe just a little?"

"But I have to leave day after tomorrow," Sara said. "We can't go on acting like this thing we have is going to last forever."

Julia gathered the newspapers and placed them in a pile on the floor, as if this act was needed to give her the time to think. "Well, I, for one, don't want this 'thing,' as you call it, to end."

"I don't want it to end, either, but it has to." Sara twisted the wedding ring on her finger. It was loose now that she had lost weight from the chemo. They had been in college when Grady bought it, a silver band with four small diamond chips imbedded in the band, bought from a local jeweler that his dad had sold insurance to. He had paid for it in installments.

"Sweetie, what are you thinking about? You seem a thousand miles away."

"I was thinking about Grady, actually."

"Wonderful," Julia said sarcastically. She left the bed and Sara pulled the covers close to make up for the loss of her warmth.

"Where are you going?" Sara asked.

Julia put on her red kimono and crossed the room. Her apartment was cold that morning, in contrast to the warm, inviting bed.

"I have something I want to show you," Julia said. She went into her studio and returned with a large canvas. She leaned it with its subject matter toward the wall. "I debated whether to show this to you or not," she added.

"What is it?" Sara asked.

Julia angled the canvas toward Sara, her breasts barely covered by the red robe. Julia paused and took a deep breath, as if an actor about to go onstage. It was strange to witness Julia even remotely nervous, stranger still to think that Sara was the one who was perfectly calm.

"I did a painting of you after I heard from you that first time," she said. "I wanted to capture what I remembered of you."

Sara's resolve was weakening. She readjusted Roberto and several pillows to prepare for the private showing.

"When I first saw you again, I wondered if the painting actually looked like you," Julia began again. "But more and more I think it does. Especially these last few days. I think I've captured the new you." Julia hesitated briefly, and then turned the canvas toward Sara. "Keep in mind, it isn't finished."

An image of a vibrant woman looked out over the streets of Florence. The fountain from Max and Melanie's courtyard filled the background, the statue peaking over Sara's shoulder. The woman in the painting looked too alive and beautiful to be her, even an imagined version. She held a boldness Sara had never felt she possessed. But what if this was a part of her?

"This is the kindest, most beautiful and profound thing anyone has ever done for me," Sara said softly.

Julia leaned the portrait against the wall. "Then why do you look so miserable?" Julia asked.

"I'm not miserable, I'm happy," Sara said, with a short laugh.

Julia sat next to Sara on the bed.

"What have we done?" Sara whispered.

"We did the best thing we could have done," Julia said.

"I'm not convinced that it was the best thing. Or the right thing," Sara said.

Julia paused, as though carefully forming her words. "Listen, I thought I was too old for something like this to happen," Julia said. "But I'm grateful that it did. I can't tell you how many unsatisfying relationships I've had over the years. I know this development has surprised you, Sara. But you're not the only one who's surprised."

"But I can't stay here forever," Sara said. "I have to go back home. I have to go back to Grady."

Julia looked as though Sara's words had slapped her in the face. "As naïve as this sounds, darling, I haven't given a thought to your leaving."

"I don't have the luxury of being naïve." Sara sounded colder than she intended.

They didn't speak for several seconds. Roberto's raspy purr accompanied their silence. Julia turned away, facing the portrait Sara was convinced she could never live up to.

"It doesn't matter," Julia said, matching Sara's coldness. She stood and walked into the bathroom.

Sara followed her, spewing apologies.

Julia turned to face her. "Why are you apologizing?" she asked. "You're allowed to say what you need to say. I'm just surprised that you returned to reality before I did."

Sara leaned into the doorframe as Julia washed her face in the sink and dried it with a towel. The thought occurred to her that she could watch Julia do this simple task every day for the rest of her life. But thoughts like these were too painful to pursue. How did she get herself in this mess? She saw now her naiveté in wanting more out of life.

"I just can't bear getting any closer to you," Sara said. "It already feels like I'll have to rip my heart out in order to leave."

"May I remind you that your heart isn't the only heart affected," Julia said somberly.

"I can't believe how quickly I've managed to screw things up," Sara said.

"Spare me the martyr act," Julia said.

Their reflections in the bathroom mirror revealed a non-traditional picture of what she had always thought love to be. Her world had flipped upside down. What used to make sense now made no sense at all. What she had thought was love all along, was some sort of misguided form of comfort. Real love, she had discovered only recently, wasn't comfortable at all. It was riddled with exposure and risks. Things Sara had expertly avoided most of her life.

Julia rubbed lotion onto her face and hands as regret filled Sara.

We could be making love right now, she thought, *muffling their screams so that the Biraldi's wouldn't hear.*

But did Julia really think that she would leave Grady? Sara followed Julia into the bedroom. The portrait sat against the wall like a witness to her ineptness. That woman was a stranger, an image impossible to live up to. She would never be that confident, that beautiful.

"How can I fix this?" Sara asked.

From her ornate wooden wardrobe, Julia chose a gray blouse and blue jeans and tossed them onto the bed.

"Nothing broken. Nothing to fix," she said curtly.

Sara's mind scrambled for the right things to say, but came up empty. Julia tossed her robe onto the bed, putting on a black bra and panties.

"Do you have any idea how good you look naked?" Sara said, breaking her own need to be serious.

Julia shot her a look. "Don't do that to me," she said, as she finished dressing. "I need to go to the market. Francesco and Georgio are coming over for dinner tonight, remember?"

Francesca was Julia's friend who owned a dress shop in Florence. Georgio was her boyfriend from the university. "I look forward to it," Sara said, which wasn't really true. She didn't look forward to anything at that moment. Looking forward had been one of the reasons she had created this mess. She had wanted to make the most of whatever time she had left but she hadn't realized what that might entail. Life, she had come to realize yet again, was incredibly messy when you jumped right into it with both feet.

Julia returned the canvas to her studio. Sara instantly missed the woman she might have become if she weren't such a coward. But at the same time she felt relieved that she didn't have to live up to her anymore. She followed Julia into the kitchen.

"Please don't be angry with me," Sara said.

"I'm not angry. I'm just very disappointed. And I don't want to talk any more right now." Julia ground up fresh coffee beans in the grinder, their aroma filling the room. She brought the glass coffee pot from the cabinet.

"Can we talk more later?" Sara asked.

"Well, if we wait long enough, you'll already be gone."

"Ouch," Sara said. "I guess I deserved that."

In the last week, Sara had had glimpses of Julia as a powerful attorney, her career for most of the time they had been apart. She had seen the cold toughness that would be required of her in that job. It was still in her. A part of her. Of course.

"I seem to have a knack for saying things people don't want to hear," Sara said.

"Let's just put this behind us," Julia said. She paused a beat. "So what do you want to do today?"

"If I'm the master at apologizing, you're the master at changing the subject."

"Well, let me do what I'm good at, okay?" Her hazel eyes had darkened.

Sara stopped herself from apologizing again.

"I'll go do the shopping. You can hang out here if you want," Julia said.

Any other day Julia would have invited Sara to go shopping with her. But she could understand her need to be alone. "Actually, I think I'll explore a little of Florence on my own."

"Fine by me," she said, no emotion in her voice.

Sara felt horrible. If only she had kept her thoughts to herself. She returned to the bedroom and dressed in black pants and a taupe blouse. As an afterthought, she wrapped the red scarf loosely around her shoulders. At first the color had been shocking to her, but now it hardly seemed vibrant enough. She added a light coat of lipstick from Julia's collection in the bathroom that matched the scarf. What she had once thought was extravagant, now seemed necessary.

Sara made up the bed, carefully lifting Roberto to smooth out the sheets underneath. "I'm envious," she whispered. "You get to stay in Julia's bed as long as you want." Sara smoothed out his whiskers; his eyes closed. On the way to the kitchen she stopped to pet Bella lying on a sofa cushion. She didn't run—a small victory. Sara thought of Luke. Would he put up with a cat if she got one when she got back?

When Sara returned to the kitchen Julia was whisking eggs in a bowl. "Would you like an omelet?" she asked. Her emotions from before had smoothed out like the wrinkled sheets in the bedroom.

"Yes, thank you." Sara poured two glasses of juice and thought how unusual it was for someone to make her breakfast. When they were young, the children always made her eggs and toast on Mother's Day; the toast blackened to a carcinogen.

"I didn't mean to screw up our morning," Sara said. "I guess everything was just too perfect."

"It's okay, darling. We're in the deep end now; let's just try to stay afloat, shall we?"

Sara nodded.

They finished breakfast and the phone rang. Julia answered it, and then covered the receiver with her hand. "It's Melanie. Do you mind if I talk?"

"Of course not," Sara said.

Julia took the phone into the living room while Sara finished her omelet. Minutes later she found Julia on the sofa petting Bella. She waved a goodbye before leaving the apartment, and felt relieved when Julia returned the wave.

Sara had only been in Italy a few days, but felt comfortable finding her way around Florence. She walked toward the center of town as sunlight claimed the sidewalk in front of her. The buzz of motor scooters filled every corner of Florence, like bees buzzing out of a hive.

The city is incredibly alive, Sara thought. *Florence being yang to Siena's yin.*

On one of the side streets Sara stopped inside the open doors of a church. In seconds she moved from bright sunshine to the dark, cool, ancient sanctuary. She covered her head with her scarf, tying it under her chin as another woman was doing just inside the door. The walls were stone, accented with rich, dark wood and lined with stained glass windows. A few people were milling around, looking at the different statuary and paintings. They whispered their comments out of respect for the sacred quiet. Footsteps, overpowering the voices, echoed through the corridor. An alcove to the left was lit up with hundreds of small candles. A bigger, more ornate version of the Mary in the fountain at Max and Melanie's towered above her.

Sara deposited a euro in a wooden box nearby and lit one of the remaining candles. She kneeled, thinking she should pray, but uncertain of what she should pray for. Forgiveness? Healing? Courage? Her life seemed too complicated for even God or sacred virgins to figure out and so she just allowed her thoughts to rest.

After several minutes she stood, bowed awkwardly, and made her way back to the open doors. The bells began, announcing a clear, steady heartbeat of the city. Sara stopped in the archway and closed her eyes. She let the bell's vibration ring in her body; the heartbeat of Florence mingling with her own.

For the remainder of the afternoon Sara explored the ancient streets of Florence. She eventually found herself at the city wall. As she had realized in Siena, she was quite good at putting up walls herself. Psychological ones, as effective as any manmade fortress. She had started to build the wall, stone by stone, when her mother died. Now, this many years later, the walls had become a fortress. For however briefly, Sara had allowed Julia inside. But that morning, she had managed to blockade the massive doors to guard against further damage.

When Sara returned to Julia's apartment it was late afternoon. Jazz music played softly on the CD player in the living room and she was humming along in the kitchen and preparing dinner. When Sara entered the kitchen Julia smiled and to Sara it felt like the sun had returned after a long, hard rain.

"Hi, darling. Did you have a nice afternoon?" Julia was wearing her robe again and her hair was wrapped up in a towel after showering. The robe fell off her shoulder on one side, leaving the artistry of her neck exposed. When had Sara started to notice these things?

"My afternoon was good," Sara said. "How about yours?" How many times had she asked Grady for information about his day and not really wanted to know? Yet, she waited with anticipation to hear what Julia might say.

"I talked to Melanie for a long time," Julia said. "Then I went to the market." She sliced a large zucchini into thin strips.

"Can I help with anything?" Sara stepped closer and smelled the scented body lotion Julia used.

"No, I've got it covered," Julia said. "I think we'll have fun tonight. Francesca and Georgio are sweet together."

"I have to admit I feel a little selfish of our time," Sara said.

"Me, too, Sweetie, but I had already arranged this before we..." Julia smiled again. "If it's any consolation they probably won't stay late. They have work and classes tomorrow."

"You'll like Francesca, I think," Julia continued, "and Georgio is equally nice. He's getting an advanced degree in mathematics. You two have teaching in common."

Sara sat at the kitchen table. She had forgotten all about teaching and returning to her lackluster job at Beacon High. The sound of the knife on the cutting board added a sharp percussion line to the soft jazz piano playing in the background.

"I've been thinking a lot about what you said this morning," Julia said. She turned to face Sara, the knife still in her hand.

"Are you going to use that?" Sara asked, pointing to the knife.

Julia grinned and disarmed herself. "This morning was a slight misunderstanding," she said. "I assumed our feelings for each other had changed things. But I was wrong. And since you're the one in a committed relationship, I guess I have to respect whatever you decide."

Sara glanced out the window into the courtyard below. The words *committed relationship* struck a dissonant chord. Twenty-five years of marriage did constitute a committed relationship, she supposed. But what if you were absolutely bored to death with each other? Of course, she couldn't speak for Grady, but maybe that was one of the reasons he had had an affair two years before. Sara inhaled her sadness.

"What's wrong? You look awful," Julia said.

"I don't want to leave," she said softly.

Julia walked over and leaned her shoulder against Sara's, as if to steady them both. The jazz pianist improvised the melody in a minor key. "Maybe this is absolutely the wrong thing to say," Julia began. "But I think you should consider not going back."

"You can't be serious," Sara said. In her imagination Sara heard the city gate close and latch, Julia on the other side. "I have to go back," she said. "I don't have a choice."

"Of course you have a choice." Julia seemed to be gaining the strength Sara felt she was losing. "You can stay here with me. We can see where this might take us."

Sara broke their connection and sat at the kitchen table. Julia's invitation threw her into a tailspin of pleasure and guilt. The judgment and fear that had all but disappeared when they first got together now returned with the force of a tsunami.

"Loving you is wrong," Sara began, teaming with the critical voice that she hated. "It doesn't matter if it feels absolutely right. Not only am I married to Grady, but I'm married to my old life. End of story."

"This seems like emotional suicide," Julia said, not hiding her disappointment.

"Maybe if I was brave like you, Jules. But I'm not brave. Besides, I don't deserve to be this happy."

"Listen to yourself," Julia said. "Since when are you up for victim of the year? I guess it's understandable after all you've been through, but aren't you getting tired of it?"

A landslide of anger, fear and sadness vied for Sara's attention. Julia was the only person in Sara's life who she could count on to tell her the truth, even if it was about herself. But she wasn't always thrilled to hear it. A knock at the door startled them both.

"That must be Francesca and Georgio," Julia said. "God, I'm not even dressed yet. We'll have to talk about this later." Julia took off her apron and draped it on the hook behind the kitchen door. "It won't be the first time I've greeted them at the door in a kimono."

Sara went into the bedroom to freshen up while Julia greeted their guests. Julia's laughter filled the apartment and sent an ache through Sara that was only just beginning to take root. Georgio's voice sounded robust, foreign; an added bass to Julia and Francesca's treble. Sara sat on the bed trying to gather those parts of her that were spiraling out of control. She didn't have the energy for new people, but she also didn't want to disappoint Julia.

You can do this, she said to herself. *You're good at pretending nothing's wrong.*

Julia came into the bedroom and quickly got dressed, and then went into the bathroom to start on her hair. "They're opening a bottle of wine. Could you take in the brie and crackers? They're on the kitchen table."

"Of course." Sara joined her in the bathroom and applied another light layer of Julia's lipstick that matched her scarf.

"You look beautiful," Julia said, kissing her lightly on the lips. Sara took a quick look in the mirror. Despite her current crisis her face looked lighter, younger. If she weren't so miserable, she'd have to admit she looked the happiest she had ever been.

Sara took a deep breath and walked into the living room where an attractive younger couple sat waiting. She had told herself initially not to like them too much or they would be something else she would have to leave behind. But this was going to be harder than she thought.

Chapter Eighteen

Georgio stood and introduced himself and then kissed Sara's hand. He was a teddy bear of a man, perhaps early 30s, dark hair, a bit round, and inviting in his persona.

Francesca shook Sara's hand and said, "Nice to meet you."

She wore sophisticated fashions—elegant and understated, impeccably accessorized. Sara wondered if Melanie had been to Francesca's shop because there was a similarity in the way they dressed.

"What a beautiful scarf," Francesca said.

Sara smiled, but the moment felt bittersweet. The scarf, as well as the new life, would have to go in two short days. Sara served the brie and crackers and seconds later Julia entered the room. The conversation suspended momentarily, as though Julia's beauty had caught them all by surprise.

Julia sat on the plush sofa and patted the cushion next to her for Sara to join her. Sara gave a quick nod no, and chose an arm chair across the room. Francesca lifted an eyebrow.

Had Julia told them anything? Surely she wouldn't, Sara thought, *not without asking her first.*

But the intimacy of her gesture was obvious.

"Julia must be keeping you quite entertained," Francesca said to Sara. "We haven't seen her in days."

"Yes, my visit has been quite eventful," Sara said.

Julia had been watching Sara ever since they sat down. Sara purposely did not look in Julia's direction. Francesca studied them for several seconds, her curiosity knitted in her eyebrows, and then her eyes widened slightly, as if her intuition had revealed what Julia had not confided.

"Am I missing something?" Georgio asked, as if suddenly aware of the overabundance of innuendo in the room.

"Of course not, darling." Francesca patted him on the arm. It was evident that she was on to them and was not so much shocked with the revelation as pleased.

"Francesca attended Bryn Mawr," Julia said to Sara.

"Yes, of course," Sara said. "No wonder your English is so good."

Francesca smiled. Bryn Mawr was a liberal all-women's college in the States, so Sara doubted she could be shocked by anything. Francesca shared some stories of her school days and Georgio spoke of his current graduate work in mathematics.

The evening progressed. The conversation was intelligent, yet also lighthearted and after dinner they lingered at the table over dessert and coffee. Despite her hesitation, Sara relaxed and warmed to Julia's friends.

Throughout the evening, Sara and Julia exchanged longer and deeper glances. By the end of dessert, Sara was ready for Francesca and Georgio to leave so she could get Julia into the bedroom. At the same time a lingering heaviness prevailed, like the humidity in New England after a hard summer rain.

They spent the majority of the next day in bed and by late afternoon took tea and pastries to the balcony. Sara was to leave for the airport early the next morning. Julia had arranged to borrow Georgio's Fiat to drive Sara to Milan. As the time of her departure neared, Sara found herself withdrawing more and more.

"Are you okay?" Julia asked her.

"I suppose," she said, picking at a croissant.

Julia put her hand on Sara's.

"You have an artist's hands," Sara said. "Strong, yet feminine at the same time. I'll miss your hands," she added. "Actually, I'll miss every inch of you."

Julia smiled briefly. "I'm not sure how to do this."

"Do what?"

"Say goodbye." Neither looked in the other's eyes. "I usually can't wait to get rid of someone," Julia said. "But this has definitely been different."

"Maybe I could visit again next year," Sara said, but she didn't even know if there would be a next year. She had told Julia about the cancer scare but she had not told her it was back. She wondered now if it was wise to keep it from her.

"I don't know if I can go that long without seeing you," Julia said. "I could come to the States. I haven't been for a visit in quite a while. And I've been wondering if there's a market for my paintings there."

"What about Grady?" Sara asked.

"Yes, what about Grady?" Julia's question felt pointed and meant to challenge.

"I'm sure he'd be happy to see you," Sara said, not up for the challenge.

Julia laughed briefly. Sara hadn't asked what had happened between Julia and Grady before they had parted thirty years before.

But the last thing she wanted to talk about at that moment was Grady.

"I don't know what you want," Julia said. "Do you want me to leave you alone? Do you want to pretend this never happened?"

"In a way, I do wish it had never happened," Sara said.

"Excuse me?" Julia asked.

"That didn't come out right," Sara said. "I just don't like pain," Sara added. "And leaving you feels like the most painful thing I'll ever do."

On the opposite balcony, Mrs. Baraldi came out to gather the laundry. Their conversation ceased. Mrs. Baraldi nodded her greeting as the clothesline squeaked steadily with each pull of her hands. What would Julia's Italian neighbor think of the dramatics in the apartment across the way? Sara wondered.

But every family had its dirty laundry. At some point over the last two weeks, Julia had relayed the story of Mrs. Biraldi's brother, a priest, who had a mistress and a brood of children all looking exactly like him; his vow of chastity left at the altar like an abandoned bride. But Sara imagined that if revealed the American artist in love with another American woman could keep the grapevine of her extended family producing wine for weeks.

Bella rubbed her face against Sara's leg and startled her out of her thoughts. It was a bold move for Bella to come out on the balcony and Sara leaned down and rubbed under her chin to reward her. When Sara looked up Julia had gone.

Sara went inside to look for her and knocked lightly on the closed bedroom door. Sara was reminded of their first morning at Max and Melanie's. They seemed to be talking to each other through doors these days.

Julia invited her in and Sara joined her at the window. The narrow streets bustled with activity. Yet Florence felt desolate at that moment. Neither spoke. It was as if the sadness between them had no voice. In Sara's mind they had reached a dead end in their relationship. The road before them had no way forward. It could only wrap back around to the same place.

"At least we had this week," Sara offered meekly.

Julia's face tensed. "Sara, you are driving me insane! One minute this is the best thing that's ever happened to you. Then next minute you wish it had never happened. Make up your mind, Sweetheart, what do you want?"

"I want you," Sara said, without hesitation. "I want to stay here forever. Whatever *forever* is."

"Then why don't you stay?"

"And do what?"

"I'm sure they need teachers here, too," Julia began. "Especially English-speaking ones. Besides, I have enough money to support us both for a while."

Sara had money, too. Even after the trip, the money she received for Mimi's ring could support her for months. But life didn't involve a *happily ever after*. At least not her life.

"Don't do this," Sara said.

"I don't like how you can just throw us away," Julia said.

"I don't want to talk about this." Sara sounded like Grady. Practicality trumped dreams.

"Why not?" Julia insisted. "Why not talk about it?"

"Because it will just make everything worse," she said.

"What are you so afraid of, Sara?"

Julia's question penetrated her. "What am I afraid of?" she asked. "Getting hurt, of course. Hell, even life terrifies me. Maybe someone with more courage would consider the different options and maybe even stay here. But I'm not that person, Julia. I wish I was. But I'm not." The tears had begun now.

Julia's face softened. Sara sat on the bed, hugging a box of tissues to her chest to clean up her messy downpour. Julia sat next to Sara and put an arm around her. Their sadness rocked them, like two trees quaking in a storm. Losses crackled through Sara, like bolts of lightning crashing to earth. Her mother's death. Her father's absence after she died. The day Julia had left, when they were sixteen. Her marriage to Grady and all their disconnections over the years. And then the cancer. The cancer diagnosis had been a blessing and a curse. It had woken her up from the deep sleep she had been living. Cancer had taught her that life was finite. That every moment deserved her attention and was a miracle in itself. But it hadn't taught her everything. It hadn't taught her how to take responsibility for her life.

"I need you to understand something," Sara said to Julia after her tears had slowed. "This isn't a piece of cake for me, either. I don't know how I'm going to get through the next twenty-four hours as it is. Do you think I don't realize what I'm doing? Or how much I'm hurting us both?"

A pile of used tissues formed a mountain between them. "I don't understand why you would go back to such an unsatisfying life," Julia said.

Sara wiped a lone tear that ran down her cheek. The drama that had played out between them seemed an eternal conflict. Would she follow the dictates of the heart or those of the mind?

Despite Sara's cathartic outpouring, it felt obvious which path she would take. Her Puritan ancestors now had a chorus of voices cheering from the sidelines of her mind, telling her to do the right thing, the appropriate, acceptable thing.

"Do you really want to know why I'm doing this?" Sara asked finally, her voice soft with surrender. "Because this is what I do, Julia. I don't have the guts to choose anything else. I can't change my whole life and start over. I don't know how to do something like that. I'm surprised I even allowed myself to love you in the first place."

"Are you saying what happened between us was a mistake?" Julia asked.

"No, it wasn't a mistake. I just wish I were a different person."

"But you could be if you just tried," Julia said.

Could she? She wanted to believe Julia but she felt at odds with herself, as if her old and her new life were in a tug-of-war with each other. And at that moment, her old life was winning.

"You're asking too much from me," Sara began again. "I have Grady to think about and my children. If they found out about our last week together, they'd think I'd gone completely nuts." She attempted a laugh but it sounded more like a wail. "You have to realize, Julia, that I've spent my whole life living out the expectations of other people. That's what I do. I'm not supposed to have a life. I'm not supposed to go to a foreign country and fall in love with someone. Not just someone but a woman, for Christ's sake. And then live happily ever after? Who does that kind of thing?"

"You do," Julia said.

Sara lay on the bed. Julia joined her. They didn't speak for several minutes. "I need some time," Sara said finally.

The room darkened. Thunder rumbled in the distance. They lay together staring at the ceiling like two bodies washed and laid out for burial. Their perfect time together had come to an end. This poignant moment called for something more. Professional mourners, Sara decided. A chorus of wise Italian women wearing black and beating their breasts in anguish. But there was no one to witness the passing of what could have been. She had asked Julia for more time but was time what she needed?

By noon the next day they stood at the busy airport in Milan waiting for the time when Sara would have to leave. "So you'll email?" Julia asked.

"Yes, of course," Sara said, distracted by the movement around them.

"You know, there is this little invention called telephones, too," Julia said.

Sara looked at her watch. Would Jess remember to pick her up at the airport in New York? All morning Sara had focused on the details of her flight: the timing of getting to the airport, making sure she hadn't forgotten anything, departure times and arrivals, numbers of gates. These things helped her avoid the temptation to stay, which had been growing all day.

"Do you think the plane will be on time?" Sara asked. She was taking chit-chat to a whole new level in an attempt to avoid a dramatic goodbye. At any moment she might begin to spout off about the weather.

"They usually are on time," Julia said.

"At least the weather's good." Sara cringed. The small talk was driving her mad, but she deserved madness, didn't she?

"Max and Melanie called while you were in the shower this morning," Julia said. "They wanted to wish you a good flight."

"That's nice." Sara felt distant, as though a part of her—the cowardly part—had already left to board the plane.

Her motives for going back to Grady and her old life were not something Sara trusted Julia to understand. She felt like a prisoner given day leave, who now must return to her cell to finish out a life sentence. It wasn't rational, but it was the way she felt. Her only regret was how her irrationality had affected Julia.

Two teenage girls with backpacks thrown over their shoulders spoke in animated Italian next to them. Sara wondered where they were going and what adventure they had in store. She turned to Julia and smiled.

"What?" Julia asked.

"They remind me of us," she said. "We were going to back-pack around Europe, remember?"

"We still could," Julia said.

Sara ignored her comment. "I wonder what might have happened if you hadn't moved away."

Julia and Sara watched the girls intently. "Funny how some-thing so long ago can be so vivid," Julia said. "I can still remember the day I left Northampton."

"You waved at me from the cab as you drove away," Sara said. "My heart was breaking."

"Mine, too," Julia said softly. "Kind of like now."

Sara glanced at her watch to avoid looking at Julia. "I have to go," she said, with an urgency that suggested the plane was already roaring down the runway. Sara grabbed her travel bag and purse and a copy of the *New York Times* she had bought in the airport to read on the way home. They turned for a final, quick embrace. Sara held her breath as they embraced, as though Julia's scent might weaken her.

"Wait a minute," Julia said. She pulled a small wrapped gift out of the side pocket of her purse.

"What's this?" Sara asked.

"Just a little going-away present," Julia said.

Sara tucked the package into her travel bag. "Thanks for everything," she said, sounding like a lodger acknowledging the hospitality of a stranger.

"You're welcome." Julia's words sounded guarded. "This is when I beg you to stay, right?"

"Please don't," Sara whispered. She turned away, her steps quickening as she approached the gate. She didn't look back. She didn't wave. She couldn't bear to. It was taking every ounce of her strength to leave.

Within seconds Sara had disappeared into airport security, and out of Julia's life.

Chapter Nineteen

Sara leaned into the window letting her body absorb the vibration of the plane readying to take off. Her emotions disappeared into the steady drone of the engines. As they lifted off and climbed through the clouds the plane began to bounce against the wind currents. Her stomach leapt to her throat. It seemed appropriate that there would be turbulence. Turbulence that was serious enough to make her wish she had Julia to hold onto in that fatal last tailspin to the earth.

An attractive older woman in her 70s was sitting next to Sara. She pulled an elegant rosary from her large purse. The Madonna again. In this incarnation, she was surrounded by gold and pearls and hanging from a gold chain. The older woman closed her eyes, the gold Mary resting among the wrinkles of her hands. For some reason this comforted Sara.

They climbed in altitude until the turbulence finally ended. Sara and the woman exchanged relieved smiles. Then she returned the gold Madonna to an inner compartment of her purse, and pulled out a book to read, as if her mission to keep them safe had ended.

A plane crash would have at least ended my misery, Sara thought.

She welcomed the thought of not having to deal with herself anymore.

"Are you all right, dear?" the older woman asked. Her hair was white and had a sophisticated cut. She was obviously older but at the same time appeared to defy age. Sara had assumed she was Italian, but her soft accent sounded like someone from the southern United States, possibly New Orleans.

"I've been better, I guess," Sara said. Something about this woman made her want to open up. She was everyone's ideal grandmother. Soft, welcoming; someone who would always have homemade chocolate chip cookies in the cookie jar.

"Your trip didn't go so well?" the woman asked.

"Oh no, it was wonderful," Sara said softly. "But I have to go home now." Her determination to return to Grady and her old life felt fragile now, as if based on a false sense of duty. She had traveled five thousand miles to reinforce her allegiance to the rule books of life. Rule books that charted out safe, well-traveled courses, where there was no room for unexpected surprises or life-altering decisions.

"It doesn't sound like you really want to go home," the woman said.

Her eyes were blue with flecks of brown.

They were kind eyes, Sara thought, *with no judgment in them.*

The fact that Sara would probably never see this woman again invited the truth.

"I fell in love with someone there," Sara confessed. "I didn't plan on it. It just happened."

The woman nodded, as if in touch with some deep understanding.

"I did the right thing by ending it," Sara said. "It was the thing that would cause the least damage and disruption to my life. People count on me not to change, you know?"

The woman sighed. "That must have been very hard for you," she said.

"It was horribly hard. But I think I've just fooled myself," Sara said. "What I thought would cause the least damage to my family has caused massive injury to me. Not to mention its effect on the person I fell in love with."

A splitting headache echoed Sara's conflict. Instead of relieving the pain with the aspirin in her purse, she let it punish her.

Waves of desperation washed over Sara as she stared into the clouds contemplating how to reenter her old life. "In Italy, I found the life I always dreamed of," she added softly.

The woman reached over and patted Sara's arm. Her touch was warm and soft.

"You're so kind to listen to me," Sara said.

"I wish I had some wisdom for you, dear," the woman said. "Love is difficult. But at the same time it's what makes living bearable."

Sara looked over. There was compassion in the woman's eyes. It felt odd confiding in this stranger. But at the same time it felt like an unexpected gift to have the woman there. Was this what it was like to have a mother who was still alive? This thought saddened her more. A part of her wanted to sob in this kind stranger's arms. But Sara would not allow herself that option. She thanked the woman again for listening and took out her newspaper. She offered the woman part. The woman declined, pointing to her book. Sara pretended to read as the words blurred from the tears she would not allow to fall.

Later in the flight, as the older woman dozed, Sara reached into her travel bag and pulled out the small package from Julia.

Inside was a framed photograph of the two of them together on their last day in Siena. Julia had insisted Max take a photo of them in their courtyard in front of the fountain. Sara was wearing the red scarf now packed away in the deep recesses of her luggage. They stood by the fountain, their arms around each other. Julia was glancing over at Sara with a look of genuine love and affection. Sara could not remember anyone ever looking at her that way. And this had been before they had consummated their relationship. Had Julia known what would happen between them?

Sara's demeanor in the photograph radiated happiness. The woman in stone peaked out from behind; her arms outstretched and embracing them. Sara closed her eyes to shut out the memory and put the photograph away. At that moment if she could have turned the plane around she would have.

Hours later the plane landed at JFK airport. Sara followed the steady stream of passengers from her flight through security and customs. The older woman and Sara embraced before departing.

"I'm sure you'll do the right thing," the woman said.

"But what is the right thing?" Sara asked.

"Love," she said.

Two women, smiling and happy, about Sara's age, waved at the older woman when they came up the escalator. "Those are my daughters," the woman said.

They parted and Sara thought of the Madonna in the inner recesses of the woman's purse, the mother to mothers. Sara would miss this woman and she didn't even know her name.

Jess was to meet Sara where she had dropped her off. Sara anticipated that Jess would be late. Jess was always late. Afterwards, Sara would go to Jess' apartment and sleep on the gray, lumpy couch Jess had bought used, that smelled like dogs and stale beer. Sara would feign jet lag and a headache and Jess would undoubtedly leave her alone.

Maybe there will even be something in the refrigerator for a change besides frozen dinners, Sara thought.

Not that she particularly felt like eating. Then tomorrow she would catch the train the rest of the way home, giving her time to come up with a game plan of how to reenter her life.

Sara passed through security and followed the signs to luggage claim. A man walked toward her. The familiarity of his gait caused Sara to take a second look. She stopped in the middle of the steady stream of foot traffic.

"Grady? What are you doing here?"

"I thought I'd surprise you." He wrapped his arms around Sara and gave her a quick, hard squeeze. "You definitely look surprised."

Sara fought to regain her sense of equilibrium, despite the feeling that she was falling off the edge of the world. Her survival instincts raced forward to head off a sense of intense panic. It was too early to face Grady. She needed time to fortify her defenses.

"I thought Jess was picking me up," she said. "At least that was the plan when I left. Is she all right?"

"She's fine," Grady said. "I told her I wanted to do it." Grady grabbed her travel bag that she had lugged on and off of trains throughout Tuscany and threw it effortlessly over his shoulder. "You look good, Sara. Really good."

She forced a smile.

"So how was your flight?" he asked.

His cheerfulness, in staggering contrast to Sara's grief, gave the scene a surreal quality.

"My flight was very long," she said. In truth, it felt as though she had kept the plane airborne for hours through her own efforts. "But I sat next to an interesting woman."

Sara lengthened her stride to keep up with Grady, willing her body to carry on despite her exhaustion. Why was he always in such a hurry to get places?

At luggage claim Sara and Grady waited for the first pieces of luggage to emerge from the plane. They waited in silence, allowing Sara more time to gather her thoughts. But her thoughts refused to be gathered. They were everywhere, scattered between Italy and the States like lost luggage in route to wayward destinations.

"So how was Italy?" Grady asked. His attempt to jumpstart the conversation seemed as odd as the situation.

"Italy was great," Sara said. Would he ask her about Julia? A rush of distress registered in her stomach as nausea.

"I shouldn't have given you such a hard time about going," he said. "Whatever the cost, it was obviously a great thing for you to do. You look terrific." He paused. "So, how's Julia? As beautiful as ever?"

"Yes," Sara said. "She sends you her best." She lied.

They retrieved her bag and walked toward the parking garage. Grady added bits and pieces of conversation where Sara would have preferred their usual silence. What had gotten into him? Had wandering around their empty house made him realize how much he counted on another person being there?

"I have a surprise for you," Grady announced, when they reached the car.

Sara tried to hide her lack of enthusiasm. She had had enough surprises in Italy to satiate the need forever.

"We've got reservations at the Roosevelt."

Sara smiled to hide her sadness. The Roosevelt Hotel was where they had spent their honeymoon.

"I thought it would be a nice treat for us, since we haven't seen each other for a while."

It was so unlike Grady to plan a romantic evening. Sorrow burrowed into her until she felt hollow. She forced herself not to think of the last week with Julia. She didn't know how she was going to get through the rest of the evening, not to mention the rest of her life.

They went to dinner at a small Italian restaurant near the hotel. The last thing Sara wanted was Americanized Italian food, but she didn't have the strength to object.

"Is there something wrong?" Grady asked at dinner. "You're not yourself."

It must be bad if even Grady senses something, she thought.

"It's jet lag, I guess." Sara took a sip of water, offering a faint smile to appease him. Externally, she carried on. Internally, her regrets screamed at her that she was having dinner with the wrong person.

"How about I rub your shoulders when we get back to the room." Grady took her hand. Sara pulled it away before she realized what she had done. "What's with you, babe?"

"Nothing," she said. *Everything,* she thought. "I just don't know how affectionate I'll be tonight, Grady. I really am very tired."

"Right," he said curtly, and then self-corrected to a kinder tone. "Let's just have a quiet evening then, and we'll head back home in the morning."

"Thank you," Sara said. He was making such an effort she felt bad for putting him off. The nausea rose. She felt like she might be sick. "I need to find the restroom. Will you order me something?"

"Sure," he said. "What do you want?"

"Anything," she said before flagging down a waiter who pointed the way to the restrooms. Behind the privacy of the stall door, the emotion that had threatened to overwhelm her since the airport in Milan rushed forward. She muffled a scream. Then the tears began: a sudden, messy flashflood of emotion.

"Are you all right?" a woman asked from the next stall.

Sara sniffed back tears, embarrassed that someone had heard her. "Yes, I'm fine," Sara said.

"Can I get someone for you?"

The woman's kindness made her tear up again. "No, really, I'm fine," she insisted. She stayed in the stall and held back the emotion until the woman left, then continued crying into a wad of toilet paper to mute her outburst. She had cried more in the last two weeks than she had cried in a lifetime. Some of the tears out of joy. Some out of sadness. She had also attracted the kindness of strangers.

Sara finished off the roll to blow her nose and then went to the sink to wash her face. The woman in the mirror looked sad, broken. Afraid to be herself.

She reapplied her makeup, relying heavily on under-eye concealer to mask the puffiness.

Sara returned to the table. "Sorry I took so long."

"No problem," Grady said, buttering a roll. He didn't notice the devastated woman sitting across from him. "I ordered you lasagna."

"Great," she said half-heartedly.

"I haven't eaten all day," Grady said. "I just had a pack of peanuts at the airport. I've been looking forward to a steak all day."

Restaurants brought out the carnivore in Grady. He became like his father, who ate meat and potatoes every night.

"How was traffic?" Sara asked, as if the question were important.

"Not bad for a weekend," he said. "The kids say hello, by the way. They still can't believe you actually went to Italy. Oh, and John and Ashley want to have us to their new apartment for dinner."

John had announced his engagement to Ashley last Christmas. They had met in law school and were waiting until they graduated to get married. Ashley was just the type of woman Sara imagined John would end up with. She came from a wealthy New England family and was both beautiful and brilliant. Money and beauty mattered to John.

"They're living together?" Sara asked. "Since when?"

"Last week," he said. "John talked to me about it. They've got another year before they're through with law school, and they can save money for a house by sharing expenses."

"I guess that makes sense," she said. Their oldest son had already chosen an expected course, one approved of by his father. "Are her parents okay with it?"

"They weren't at first. But they seem to have come around."

As Grady and Sara continued to talk, her headache subsided and she began to feel more normal. If all else failed, they could always talk about their children. This common interest filled her with unexpected gratitude.

Back at the hotel Sara purposely took a long bath, giving Grady time to fall asleep before she came to bed. She put on the gown that she had worn very little on the second half of her trip, and slid under the cool sheets beside him.

Sara glanced at the clock by the bed. It was midnight in New York, six in the morning in Florence. In her imagination she heard the church bells ring in Julia's neighborhood. Julia would still be sleeping in the bed they had shared. Sara closed her eyes, remembering what it was like to lie beside her. For a moment she could almost feel Roberto nestled between their feet. Empty of tears, memories of Julia tormented her with their comfort until out of sheer exhaustion she fell asleep.

The next morning her headache had returned. She felt hungover with emotion and thankful for the fact that she and Grady often traveled in silence. He sat behind the wheel of his SUV with a full tank of gas and maneuvered their way out of the city.

"So tell me about Julia," Grady said when they hit the interstate.

Sara turned to look out the window. "What do you want to know?"

"Has she changed? What did she look like? What did you guys talk about?"

Since when did Grady get to be so inquisitive? she wondered. "She was the same, really," Sara said. Her voice sounded meek, pathetic. "Just a little bit older."

Grady nodded and drummed the steering wheel with his thumbs, as if his imagination was filling in the blanks. "So what did you guys do?"

The nausea from the day before returned to accompany Sara's headache. The last thing she wanted to do was talk about Julia with Grady. "Honey, can we not talk about this right now. I'm really jet-lagged."

"Sure," he said. Without skipping a beat, he set the cruise control and leaned back in his seat.

Silence settled between them as she watched the scenery out the window. Sara was reminded of the train trip between Milan and Florence. Miles of countryside had flashed by, accented by tiny towns. Scenes of being with Julia played over and over in Sara's mind creating a morose mixture of pleasure and pain. The vague longing she had had for something more in her life was now clearly defined. She knew exactly what she wanted, yet felt incapable of accepting it.

By midday, they pulled into their driveway. The house greeted Sara with its sameness. The only difference was that Grady had planted a row of honeysuckle vines along the fence and attached their runners with twine. The front flower beds were in desperate need of weeding; an unending chore. They would need to paint the outside of the house again soon. She couldn't say she was happy to be home, but there was something comforting about knowing what was expected of her there. Grady unloaded the car while she went inside.

The house seemed darker than Sara remembered. Grady brought in her luggage. "It's freezing in here," she said. "Do you have the air conditioner on?" The iciness of Sara's old life crept back into her veins.

"Yeah, it's been hotter than usual this week," Grady said. "Will you make lunch?"

Grady took their luggage to the bedroom while Sara searched the cabinets for a can of tuna. For the first time she realized that she hadn't brought Grady anything from Italy. It hadn't occurred to her. Perhaps, unintentionally, her coming back was the only gift she had to give.

Chapter Twenty

For the next few weeks emails from Julia arrived daily. Newsy emails about Italy and her paintings that revealed very little of her true feelings, as though Grady might be standing over Sara's shoulder and reading what she had written. In every letter Julia made cryptic references to their time together: *I thought of the fountain today. The bells of the cathedral are chiming the hour. Roberto misses you.* But nothing related to the intimacy they had shared. Perhaps this was Julia's way of honoring Sara's need for more time.

Sara's emails in return were dull, lifeless. She hid her feelings from Julia as completely as she hid them from herself. She lived in purgatory, suspended between heaven and hell, between memories of Julia and her everyday reality.

Weeks passed, then months, while she waited patiently for the old Sara to return. Yet like a stretched rubber band, the old Sara refused to snap back into its original shape. Everything had changed, and nothing at all. She was purposely distant with Grady. She stayed late at school and stayed in her home office until the early hours of the morning.

Never one to push, Grady allowed the distance without questioning it. Every evening Sara wrote long emails to Julia. She sent a few, but deleted most, destroying all evidence of how she had opened a vein and let her emotions bleed red on the page.

Sara's body ached for Julia, as though it was a separate entity and every cell had memory of her. She touched herself in the shower, imagining it was Julia touching her. She listened to her breath and heard Julia's. Whenever she relived their time together, replaying scenes in her mind, Sara fell into the delicious sensuousness of their power. Instead of dying away, these embers lived on, constantly pumped by the circulation of memory.

In her imagination Julia sat by the fountain, whose patron saint had given them acceptance. The water's song remained unchanged. It flowed in eternal ringlets at the woman's feet. Candles in terracotta holders flickered through the twilight garden. Sara longed to be there with Julia as the hillside turned golden, as if illuminated from within.

Sara touched her fingers to her lips, remembering the first time she and Julia had kissed. In the evenings she went outside and glanced up at the night sky. *Star light, star bright,* she repeated, missing the partner in her duet. Sara's wish was as clear and certain as the water in the fountain, five thousand miles away.

Three months passed. Sara suffered through another round of chemo, lost her hair, vomited with regularity, but nothing felt as torturous as keeping the secret of her love for Julia.

"Are you ready to go?" Grady asked.

On Grady's birthday they always went to his parent's house to celebrate his early December birthday and since it fell on a Sunday this year his mother was going all out. She had made his favorite meal of roast beef, mashed potatoes, green beans, and an apple pie for dessert. Sara's role was thankfully small and unimportant.

Sara collected his wrapped present and joined Grady in the car. "Behave yourself today, okay?" Grady said, as she buckled up.

"What do you mean? Don't I always?"

"You've been so sullen lately. Just try to enjoy yourself for a change."

Had she been sullen? Was it that obvious? For some reason this made her feel a little better. If she was a martyr for doing the right thing, at least this hinted that some redeeming value might be found in her suffering.

They arrived at Grady's parent's house and Grady walked to the front door ahead of her. Sara mentally prepared herself for the scene to follow: greetings for the adored son, acknowledgment of the much less favored daughter-in-law, followed by pleasantries, a tough roast, banter, and goodbyes.

"Well you look good, Sara," his mother said.

"You look good, too, Stella." Sara handed her Grady's present.

Stella's hair had looked the same since Sara and Grady were children. Styled with industrial-strength hairspray, Sara doubted a bomb blast could dislodge it from its post.

Grady's birthday was Stella's production. Presents were always opened at the end of the meal. Stella handed them out to Grady as she deemed fit, shaking and making a big deal over each one, as if Grady were still in grade school.

Grady's father, Howard, gave Sara a hug. He was Grady's height of six feet, but had a bulk to him that Grady had never had. Despite the winter temperatures, he wore a green polo shirt, orange sweater and green striped pants, as if to make the moment more festive. His challenge with clothing choices, notwithstanding, Sara had always liked him.

They gathered in the dining room while Stella served lunch. Then the day proceeded following the same script as it did every year.

"How's school, Sara?" Howard asked, scooping up a spoonful of mashed potatoes.

"Fine," she said.

"What play are you doing this year?"

This was always Howard's question. "I'm not sure yet," she said.

"I still remember you in that play at Beacon. What was the name of it?"

Every year she told him the name. Every year he forgot.

"You were great in that," he said.

Sara's senior year she had played the female lead in the school play. Julia usually got these parts, but wasn't around to play it that year. The local newspaper had even written a glowing article about her performance.

"Howard, leave her alone," Stella said. "Your son gets to be the star today." She beamed at Grady. "Isn't it amazing that he's 45?" she continued. "Of course his mother is only 39."

Everyone laughed except for Sara. Sullen didn't even begin to describe her current mood. When it came time to open the gifts Grady seemed unimpressed with the digital camera Sara had bought him.

"The old one works fine," he said.

"The kids all chipped in. They said this is one of the best."

"Where did you get that old camera, anyway?" Howard asked. "Did we give it to you?"

"No, a friend did."

"Julia," I said. "And me, too, actually." It felt strange to say Julia's name.

"Julia David?" Stella asked. "Oh my, that girl was so beautiful. What ever happened to her anyway?"

I fell in love with her, Sara wanted to say.

"Some lucky guy probably snagged her up in a hurry," Howard laughed.

Stella sighed and looked at Grady, as if fate had delivered him a cruel blow by not letting him be that 'lucky guy.'

"Is the pie ready?" Grady asked his mother. His eyes met Sara's and warned her not to say anything further. Had Grady not told them it was Julia she had visited in Italy? Or maybe he had neglected to tell them that she had even been gone. Sara was a minor player in their family drama. And if left up to Stella, Sara was convinced she would be written out of the play altogether.

They were home by seven with Grady in front of the television watching a football game. Sara didn't feel like being alone and called Maggie. "I need a friend. Do you mind if I come over?"

"Not at all," Maggie said, sounding surprised by the request. "The place is a mess, but I'm sure you won't mind."

Despite their four-year friendship, Maggie had been to Sara's house only once to give her a ride home when her Volvo wouldn't start. The place had been in its usual chaotic state. Sara had been to her house once, as well, a Christmas faculty party several years before. Maggie's house was immense, too big for one person, in Sara's view. Maggie had received it in her divorce settlement from an unfaithful husband. In contrast to Sara's disorganized domain, everything in Maggie's house was placed with sterile precision.

They sat in Maggie's den in matching wingback chairs, the same color as their glasses of Merlot. Did she plan that? Sara wondered. The walls were a light shade of green. Sara looked around for the 'mess' Maggie had claimed her home was in but found nothing out of place.

Tasteful window treatments and carefully chosen furniture, each piece articulated with a green color scheme in mind, adorned the ample rooms. The books on the bookshelves were classified by category. No evidence existed of the children she herself had launched into the world except for a few immaculately matted, framed and carefully placed portrait photographs.

Sara, on the other hand, had never gotten around to putting up curtains, relying on window shades instead. Their furniture was a mixture of things they had bought in college and an eclectic collection of newer pieces that didn't quite match. Books and papers were stacked on nearly every flat surface. The dining room table and its set of matching chairs sacrificed totally to this end.

It was cold where they sat in Maggie's den. The wine provided the only warmth in the room. The plate on the side table between them held a platter with small equal squares of cheddar cheese, each pierced in the center with a green toothpick. Sara tried to imagine how many boxes of assorted color toothpicks Maggie had bought and only used the green ones. Would she perhaps donate the remainders to a catering business in town?

Sara reached for a cube of cheese.

"You said you needed a friend," Maggie said. "What's up?"

Sara thoughtfully chewed the cheese, debating what was acceptable to tell her, and swallowed. "Maggie, do you ever wish your life was different?"

"All the time," she said. "Doesn't everybody?" Maggie picked a loose thread from her olive green corduroy pants and placed it in her pocket.

"So what do you do about it?" Sara anticipated the answer. Maggie's position in life was to have no position.

"Since this cancer thing, you ask so many questions, Sara. Don't you drive yourself nuts?" Maggie smiled.

Is she comforted by the thought that she's not like me? Sara wondered.

"Yes, sometimes I do drive myself nuts." Sara pulled her sweater closer.

Maggie laughed and poured them both another glass of Merlot. Sara took a long sip and for the first time that night she felt warm. While Maggie might wish her life had played out in a different way, it would never occur to her to actually pursue another course. Perhaps this similarity was why they were friends. But Sara didn't want to be like Maggie. She didn't want to play life so safe.

"What are you thinking about?" Maggie asked. "You look like you're in a different world."

"I guess I was," Sara said. She wrapped her fingers around the wine glass as if it were a mug of something hot and she was wanting to warm her hands. She thought of Julia and another surge of warmth came. "I have a confession to make," Sara added.

"A confession?" Maggie asked. "Out with it," she added, crossing her legs. For a second, Sara could imagine what Maggie must have been like as a girl, before all the creases of her life had been ironed out. Sara imagined she was the type to seek out her adventures in books instead of real life. What would she think of Sara's adventure?

"I haven't told anyone this." Sara paused. Was she really going to tell her? This went against Sara's better judgment, but she wondered if by telling the secret it might help her to move on. But did she want to move on?

"There you go again," Maggie said. "Sara, I don't think I've ever seen you this distracted."

"Sorry," Sara said. "Maybe I shouldn't...."

"No, you can't back out now," Maggie said. "You have to tell me." Maggie waited, her green eyes expectant.

"I met someone in Italy," Sara said shyly.

Maggie sat straighter in the wingback chair. "You are kidding me," she said.

"You can't tell anyone," Sara said.

Maggie agreed. And Sara began to tell her about Julia, but a rendition of the story that Sara felt Maggie would be more inclined to accept. She told her she had met 'this person' at an art gallery and things had gone from there. She managed to tell the whole story devoid of pronouns. It was not until Maggie asked *his* name that Sara realized she would have to tell her the truth.

"Well, actually..." Sara paused and took a gulp of wine, emptying the glass. Until Italy, she had never really appreciated wine or the courage it could supply in much needed moments. But Maggie was beginning to look impatient. "Actually, it wasn't a *him* I met in Italy, but a *her*."

Sara waited for Maggie's response. At first her eyes narrowed, as if she had misunderstood, but then they widened. "You had an affair with a woman?" she whispered, as if the green walls might overhear.

Sara nodded. A part of her was pleased that she had shocked Maggie. Maybe she was different from her, after all.

"I didn't know you were gay," Maggie whispered again.

Sara spoke in her full voice. "I'm not gay."

Maggie's confusion appeared to take on a new depth.

"At least not technically," Sara added, realizing how strange this must sound. She dug the hole deeper. "At least not in terms of lifestyle. It was just a one-time thing."

Julia was the only woman Sara had ever been attracted to. For her, it wasn't about an attraction to women; it was about an attraction to Julia. But how could anyone possibly understand unless they had been through something similar? Sara was beginning to get confused, too.

"I don't know what to say." Maggie paused to arrange the remaining cubes of cheese on her plate as though circling her wagons to fend off an Indian attack.

"I guess it's too much to ask for you to be happy for me," Sara said.

"It's hard for me to see the act of adultery as a happy one," Maggie said. "You know, because of my ex," she quickly added.

The room became cold again and Maggie hadn't bothered to refill Sara's wine glass. She now regretted her confession, although she could understand her need to purge herself of the secret. But this was more than Maggie could deal with and Sara would have known that if she had stopped to think about it long enough.

"I'm sorry," Sara said.

Maggie waved her apology away and made an excuse about being tired. Sara carried the plate of cheese cubes into the kitchen while Maggie got Sara's coat, their evening ending awkwardly, at best.

On the drive home Sara contemplated Maggie's response. She anticipated their friendship would die a slow death. Sara hoped that Maggie would have enough integrity to keep her confidence. But even if she didn't, Sara doubted that her job would be in any jeopardy. Not that it would be a tremendous loss if it was.

There were things that she hadn't told Maggie. About how her love for Julia had grown stronger over these last few months instead of diminishing. How she feared she had made the biggest mistake of her life by coming back to Grady. And how it was getting harder and harder to convince herself that she had done the right thing.

Chapter Twenty-One

This was one of the most miserable Christmases of Sara's life. Topped only by the Christmas after her mother had died. But she was determined to act like nothing was wrong; as much for her sake as everyone else. Making Christmas dinner gave her a break from thinking of Julia as she preoccupied herself with the details and the timing of the meal.

Sam, their youngest son, took a small piece of turkey Sara had just taken out of the oven and blew on it before putting the morsel in his mouth. Luke, reunited with his master, watched Sam's every move, his tail beating a steady rhythm on the floor.

"Delicious," he pronounced. "You're the best, Mom." He embraced her, and then leaned down to pet Luke. Sam didn't need her anymore, a reality that made her a bit nostalgic on holidays.

"It's nice to have you home, honey," Sara said. She genuinely meant it, despite her holiday angst.

Sam was tall with sandy-colored hair that fell down into his blue eyes. A golden boy, some might call him. He had the body of an athlete, although he didn't play any sports past junior high. And during college he was handsome enough to get a job modeling men's fashions.

When Sara looked at Sam she saw not only the child she had raised who was now a young man, but also a part of herself. Unfortunately, it was a part that was insecure and overly sensitive despite his handsomeness.

"Have you had time to talk to John?" Sara asked. Since they were boys, Sam had adored his older brother. A fact that John was not always thrilled about.

"He's preoccupied with Dad," Sam said. "Plus Ashley is here so I don't know if I'll even get a chance." We now shared John with Ashley's family on holidays. They would spend Christmas morning with them before driving to her parents for the rest of Christmas day.

"How are you doing, Sam? I mean, really."

"I'm fine, Mom." He took another piece of turkey to give to Luke, and Sara playfully slapped his hand. "The new job is working out great. I don't want to stay there forever, but it's a good place to start. I can work my way up in the company if I want to, like Jess, or I can move on."

Like his father, Sam had majored in business at the University of Massachusetts, and was working at the same investment firm in New York as Jessica. She had gotten him the job starting at the lowest rung in a company where she was a few steps higher on the ladder. She was as good at looking out for her younger brother as John was at ignoring him.

"Are you dating anyone?" Sara asked. This was the question she always worked into their conversations, sometimes not as gracefully as she would like. If Sam dated, he didn't tell her about it.

"Don't worry so much." He kissed her on the cheek.

Sara didn't like how much he sounded like her. Life could totally suck, to use his words, and he would insist everything was fine. A genetic disposition, she supposed. Denial on a DNA level.

They took their places on the family stage: Sam with Sara in the kitchen; John talking with Grady; Ashley, the newest member in the cast, staying close to John; with Jessica to arrive just before the end of the first act.

"Have you talked to your sister?" Sara asked Sam. Of all the siblings, Sam was the one most likely to know what was going on with the others.

"She dumped another guy." He sampled the oyster stuffing. Jessica had brought a series of young men through their home over the years. Sara had learned early on not to get too attached to them.

"You mean the one she met at her gym?"

"Yeah, I think he's the fourth one this year. I can't even keep their names straight anymore."

"Does she talk to you about it?"

"Not really," Sam said.

Sara frowned and stirred the cranberries.

"Don't worry, Mom. Jess is just being Jess," Sam said. "She'll find somebody someday, and if she doesn't, she can just come back here to live." He chuckled.

"That phase of my life is over, dear. I have no desire to go back and do it again."

"Relax, Mom. That's the way we want it, too." Sam put his arm around her shoulder. He was easily the most affectionate of her children and the most tuned in to Sara. "So how are you, Mom? I mean, really."

Sara paused, realizing Sam was referring to her health. Which version of the story had she told him? She had downplayed the whole cancer thing with her children. As far as they knew her last round of chemo was simply routine. She was now in waiting mode again to see if the chemicals had done their job. She adjusted her wig slightly. "I'm fine, honey. Good as new."

"Are you sure?" Sam asked.

"I'm sure, honey. Honestly, I'm fine. Never been better." Sara didn't sound convincing, and he didn't look convinced. "But you're sweet to ask," she added. She caressed the stubble of his light beard and remembered a four-year-old Sam standing beside Grady in the bathroom, pretending to shave like his father. "If anything changes, I'll let you know," she reassured him.

"You just don't look that happy, Mom."

"I'm always happy," she said cheerfully.

"Come on, Mom." Sam was frowning at her.

"It's sweet of you to worry about me, honey, but I really am fine. Now go and pry John away from Dad and Ashley so you can talk to your favorite brother."

Sam kissed her on the cheek before leaving and Luke devotedly followed.

Alone again, Sara breathed deeply. She was not about to burden her twenty-two year old son with her drama. She was doing her best to play the role of faithful wife and mother.

Who am I kidding? she thought.

Not that anyone had noticed, except maybe Sam.

Their adult children had created lives of their own. They were totally familiar, and like strangers, all at the same time. They paraded past Sara and Grady year after year with new stories, new lovers, and new friends. As far as she could tell, she and Grady were expected to watch their evolution without advice or judgment, while aging gracefully on the sofa.

When Sara looked up from her pie crust, Ashley had joined her in the kitchen. "How's it going, Mrs. Stanton?"

"Fine, Ashley." Sara forced her face into a smile. "Are you having a good time?"

"Yes, Mrs. Stanton. I love watching John with his dad."

Sara's fake smile hid a very real grimace. "Ashley, please don't call me Mrs. Stanton. It makes me feel ancient." It also made her think of Stella, her stereotypical mother-in-law. Did Ashley see Sara as that out of date?

Ashley smiled a perfect smile, perhaps the result of years of orthodontia, and her blue eyes were accentuated by her blue sweater. Even when dressed in jeans she looked formal, her perfect posture matching her perfect smile.

Sara glanced down to see what she had absentmindedly put on that morning. She was dressed entirely in black—black jeans and a black turtleneck.

Molly Decker would be proud, she thought.

In her old age she was going Goth.

Her only attempt to look festive was the green Christmas ball earrings Sara wore that Maggie had given her for Christmas. A peace offering, Sara supposed, for their disastrous get-together three weeks before.

"How's law school going?" Sara asked. She used a fork to scallop the edges of the pie crust, and then placed the apple pie in the oven. Apple pies were the one dessert she knew how to make from scratch, thanks to her mother, who had made apple pies for the diner.

"The semester was rough," Ashley said. "But John and I studied like crazy to get through exams. I don't know what I'd do without him." She beamed, as if proud to have a man support her.

When Grady and Sara were engaged, they had presented a perfect picture, too, even though they didn't have a clue what marriage entailed in terms of commitment and sacrifice. But she had thought she was happy back then.

"Everything smells great, Mrs. Stanton. Can I help you with anything?"

"No, I think I've got everything under control," she said, knowing this statement wasn't the least bit true. The only thing even vaguely under control was the meal; the rest of her life was up for grabs.

"Then I guess I'll go check on John," Ashley said.

When Ashley left Sara relaxed her face and glanced at the clock. Her mind jumped time zones, something it did with growing ease. It was after midnight in Florence.

"Merry Christmas, Julia," she said softly. The words caught in her throat. Sara lowered her head and swallowed a lump of regret. She had no idea what Julia's Christmas plans might be. She had not heard from her for over a week—a fact she was determined not to worry about. She forced herself to focus on another task.

"Hi, Mom," John said.

She looked up, startled by her oldest son's sudden appearance. She stretched to hug his 6 foot 2-inch frame. He had surpassed Grady by two inches, a fact he loved to bring up in front of his dad. John reminded Sara of Grady right after college. Tall, lean, a perfectly proportioned body, a charismatic smile. He even wore his thick brown hair the same way Grady had. Short on the sides and longer on the top with an addition of a mustache he had grown the last couple of years.

"How's it going out there?" Sara asked.

"Ashley and Dad are talking about how the courts have been affected by the current administration."

"Well, I don't see how you tore yourself away," Sara said.

"Ash and I have already had that conversation a thousand times," he said. "Besides, I wanted to check on my dear, old mom."

"I like the 'dear' part, but I'm not too fond of the 'old.'"

"You know what I mean." John poured himself a tall glass of orange juice and drank half of it in the first gulp. His Adams apple was prominent like Grady's but John wasn't nearly as self-conscious as Grady had been at his age. For his entire sophomore year in high school Grady had worn turtlenecks. Nothing Sara or Julia had said to him would make him stop.

"Ashley seems to be doing well," she said.

"Yeah, she's great. And I'm really happy, Mom."

"I'm glad to hear it, honey." Sara glimpsed the boy he used to be. Confident in the direction he was going, even if others weren't.

"Have you had a chance to talk to Sam?" she asked.

"Not yet," he said. John unloaded clean dishes from the dishwasher, his job while he was growing up.

"You know how he looks up to you."

"I know, Mom. I will," his tone softened. "You know he still hasn't brought anybody home for Christmas."

"He's still young, honey, give him time. By the way, have we heard anything from your sister?"

"She called a little while ago. She'll be here soon.

"Good," Sara said. "Now go back and entertain the troops. I've got everything handled in here." She turned him toward the door and gently pushed.

Sara's oldest, most responsible child left the room, his head just below the top of the doorway. A few seconds later Grady laughed from the next room. He had settled into his role as patriarch with relish, currently holding court in the living room. Grady enjoyed being a father much more now that the children were grown. Sara supposed she enjoyed this phase more, too. Her job description had shortened considerably. Now she was to keep the family traditions going and be the person they returned to. A touchstone, of sorts, with no true needs of her own.

Sara thought of Julia and weighed the price of family traditions. But did it have to be either/or?

"Jess just drove up," Sam called from the living room.

Sara joined the welcoming committee at the front door. Their vibrant, disorganized daughter arrived juggling a briefcase, flowers, duffle bag, and excuses. Her cheeks were red from the cold and her face was framed with large silver hoop earrings. Her gray bulky sweater dwarfed her.

"Better late than never," Sam joked, getting in line for a hug.

It was only in the last few years that this tradition of embracing each other had begun. After they had ceased living together.

"Sis, you remember Ashley," John said.

"Yes, hi." Jessica shook Ashley's hand. "How's it going big brother?"

"No complaints," he said, sounding like Grady. "How about you?"

"Don't get me started," she laughed.

Jess glanced at John with what could pass for admiration. During their childhood, they would have gladly exiled the other to the outer reaches of Antarctica if given the chance. Jessica was constantly taking his things and then losing them or breaking them, totally usurping John's need for order.

"Sorry, Mom. Traffic was horrible." Jess handed Sara a bouquet of yellow roses as if a peace offering for her lateness.

"No problem, honey. I'm just glad you made it here safely."

Sara left everyone in the living room to put the roses in water and finish up dinner. At half past seven everyone gathered at their usual places around the dining room table.

"You've outdone yourself," Grady patted Sara's shoulder on the way to his chair.

By creating this moment, Sara had fulfilled Grady's dream of what their life together should be. They would grow old together, gradually adding more chairs around the dining room table as their children gathered with spouses and their children. This extension of himself, like the extension needed for the dining room table, would confirm his legacy. But why wasn't this enough for Sara?

Family gatherings always had a staged quality to her. Her father and brother had ignored the holidays after her mother died. It was a day to close the restaurant and not cook. Devoid of tradition, holidays became a day to watch sports on television and order Chinese from the one restaurant that stayed open. To this day, Sara preferred sweet and sour pork to turkey and dressing.

Any holiday traditions they observed had originated with Grady's family including a large Christmas Eve dinner and presents opened early the next morning. These events had occurred at Grady's parent's house until a few years ago, with Stella being the master of ceremonies. To move these events to their house was a hard-won battle, and was yet another thing she doubted Stella had forgiven her for. They now went over to Grady's parent's house for an elaborate Christmas brunch meant to reduce Sara's efforts to insignificance.

A perfunctory grace preceded food passed and plates filled. Everyone seemed happy. Everyone, it seemed, except Sara, who felt detached. Even though she had often thought she would give any of her children the internal organ of their choice, she also realized that she needed something more. Her guilt felt as tangible as her mother's crystal vase in the center of the table.

"The food's great, honey," Grady said.

She thanked him. Sara had barely tasted the meal that she had spent hours preparing. Months before she hadn't known if she would be allowed another Christmas. And she wasn't guaranteed next year, either. She thought longingly of Julia in her apartment, the bells tolling the hour on the quiet streets.

"What are you thinking about, Mom?" Sam asked from across the table.

"I was thinking how nice it is to see all of you together," Sara said. This was the expected answer. And everyone went on with their meal. She was invisible to them. And as long as she gave expected answers, she was responsible for her own invisibility.

Sara attempted to redeem the moment. "Actually, Sam, I was thinking about an old friend."

Sam looked up from his plate. "Sorry, Mom, did you say something?"

Voices fell silent. All eyes were on Sara. She had not anticipated this much attention, but she followed through anyway.

"You asked what I was thinking about," she said to Sam. "And what I was actually thinking about was the friend I visited in Italy."

"That's right. You've barely said anything about your trip," Jessica said.

"I didn't think you were interested," Sara said.

Until now, the grandest event of Sara's life had barely been a blip on her children's radar screen. What would they say if they knew the mousy woman in front of them had had an affair that had taken her breath away? An affair that had been so passionate, she was still trying to get over it. And that kept her up nights and tormented her.

"We've just been so busy," Sam said, "I guess we forgot to ask."

The doorbell chimed. Everyone looked toward the door. "Saved by the bell," Grady said to Sam.

"I'll get it," Sara said, welcoming an opportunity to break away from the scene. She walked the length of the hallway approaching the front door. Luke followed as official greeter. Sara opened the door, reminding Luke not to jump, and gasped when she saw who it was.

"What are you doing here?" Sara asked.

"I thought I'd surprise you." Julia smiled broadly as Sara worked to open the screen door that didn't always want to un-latch. She had asked Grady to fix it a dozen times. Sara finally pushed hard against the screen and it opened.

"Come inside," Sara said. "It's freezing out there."

"I was hoping you'd invite me in," Julia said. She stepped in-side and opened her arms. Sara hesitated before stepping into them. They embraced for several seconds until Sara realized they were not in Italy but at her front door for all of New England to see.

Sara was speechless. She couldn't decide if this was the best Christmas present of her life or the worst. "I don't know what to say," Sara said.

"How about you're glad to see me."

"I am glad to see you. But we've just started Christmas Eve dinner."

"Who is it?" Grady yelled from the dining room.

Sara's thoughts raced to problem-solve the situation.

"I'd love to meet your children," Julia said, her smile radiating calmness.

"I guess that would be okay," Sara said.

Why not? she thought. *Julia was just a friend in town who had spontaneously stopped by. No one would know what they really meant to each other, right?*

"We can do this, Sweetie." Julia squeezed Sara's hand.

Sara's knees momentarily weakened, the state they had stayed in for several days in Italy. She released Julia's hand and told herself to act normal. "I don't know whether to be angry at you or grateful," Sara whispered as they walked down the hallway.

"I vote for grateful," Julia whispered back.

Sara led Julia into the dining room. She took a deep breath. Grady stood; his expression the proverbial deer caught in headlights. "Julia?" he asked.

"Hi, Grady. Good to see you again."

Would Grady clutch his chest and drop to the floor? Sara wondered. He definitely looked that surprised.

Julia walked over and kissed him on the cheek. His face turned crimson, his Adam's apple sticking out like a white buoy in the sea of red.

"Children, this is Julia," Sara said. "Someone your father and I knew years ago. We went to high school together."

The corkscrew Grady had been holding slipped out of his hand and clanged onto the table. Grady mumbled an apology and filled his wine glass to the brim. But he looked like he could use something much stronger.

Sara introduced Julia to her children and to Ashley. Julia had a knack for winning over people quickly and from the looks on their faces, they were charmed instantly. Sam and John especially looked like schoolboys meeting a goddess. Sara could forget how captivating Julia was, until she witnessed the reactions of other people.

"Would you like some dinner?" Sara asked Julia, trying to act normal.

"If that's okay with everyone?"

Julia question was followed by unanimous nods and verbal okays, with the exception of Grady who had become the mannequin father in a holiday display case.

Sara felt sorry for him at that moment, but she didn't have the energy to take care of him. She was too busy pooling all of her psychic resources to deal with her own shock and surprise at having the third musketeer, and love of her life, arrive at their doorstep.

Sara gathered another place setting from the china cabinet and everyone shifted to make room for their unexpected guest. *Act normal*, she told herself again. *She's just a friend*. No secrets have to be revealed. Julia sat next to Sara, close enough that their legs touched. Sara pulled open the neck of her turtleneck to release some of the heat that was rising.

"Grady, pour Julia a glass of wine," Sara directed, which shook him from his stupor, at least momentarily.

"Julia's family moved away during our senior year," Sara said. "We hadn't seen each other for almost thirty years and then I visited her last summer when I was in Italy."

"You live in Italy?" Ashley asked. "John and I have talked about maybe going there on our honeymoon."

"It is a lovely place for honeymoons," Julia said. She placed her napkin in her lap and nudged Sara's leg under the table. Sara nudged her back as if warning her to stop.

"Dad, where did you and Mom spend your honeymoon?" Sam asked.

Grady looked at Sara. Could he not remember? If questioned about his name, he probably couldn't remember it, either.

"We spent a weekend in New York," Sara said. "We were saving money for this house so we didn't want to spend that much."

"Your house is lovely," Julia said.

Grady and Sara thanked her in unison, but it appeared to be the only way they were united at that moment.

"We were just asking Mom about her trip," Jessica said. "Now you both can tell us the highlights."

Sara cleared her throat and took a sip of wine to swallow her rising panic.

"You would have been proud of her," Julia said. "Your mom was practically a native. She drank wine, she explored Tuscany, and she met my friends." Julia paused.

"I surprised Julia at her art opening," Sara said, aiming for a matter-of-fact tone.

"You're an artist?" Sam asked. His adoration appeared to increase.

"A very good one," Sara said.

Julia shifted the conversation, asking about each of her children's lives. Grady was the only person at the table not thoroughly enthralled by her. His eyes stayed focused on his plate. He chewed a piece of turkey, as if it had suddenly become tough to swallow.

Dinner progressed. Sara barely ate. The scene felt like a dream that threatened to shift into a nightmare at any moment. After all her wishing to see Julia again she was suddenly there. But in her fantasies this wasn't the scenario she had had in mind. They had included linen sheets, not linen tablecloths.

Toward the end of the meal, Sam stood and held up his wine glass to make a toast. "To Mom and Dad," he said. "And to Julia," he added, beaming over at her. Grady lifted his glass but didn't drink.

After dinner Julia helped Sara clear the dishes. "Is Grady in cardiac arrest?" Julia asked when they were alone in the kitchen. "He's barely looked at me."

"What happened between you two, anyway?" Sara asked.

"It's a long story," Julia said. "Is that really what you want to talk about at this moment?" She leaned in to give Sara a kiss. Sara pushed her away.

"I forgot you hate surprises," Julia said. "But I think your kids like me."

"They adore you," Sara said. "Everybody does."

"Are you really angry at me for coming thousands of miles to see you?"

"I don't know what I am."

"Do you want me to go?"

Sara hesitated. Of course she didn't want her to go. But she couldn't reconcile her obligation to her family with her own needs. "Maybe you'd better."

Julia looked momentarily hurt, but quickly regained her composure. Sara had been so wrapped up in her own feelings she hadn't realized what this must be like for Julia.

"Will you come by and see me later?" Julia asked.

"On Christmas Eve?" There was no one she would rather spend Christmas Eve with, but she had a houseful of guests. "Where are you staying?" Sara asked.

"The B & B on Clover."

"Maybe I can come by tomorrow after Stella's brunch."

"Maybe?"

"It's just such a surprise to have you here," Sara said.

Julia leaned in to kiss Sara again and this time Sara let her. Their time in Florence flooded back in sensory memory. She had forgotten how perfectly they fit together and how soft Julia's lips were.

"God, I've missed you," Julia said softly when the kiss ended.

"I've missed you, too," Sara said. She glanced at the door. "We need to be careful, though. We wouldn't want a repeat of what happened with Melanie."

"Although that turned out all right, too," Julia said.

"But these are my children," Sara said. "What would they do if they walked in and caught their mother kissing another woman?"

"Maybe they'd applaud," Julia said.

"I doubt it," Sara countered. "Say your goodbyes and I'll try to come by to see you tomorrow." Suddenly Sara was in control of the situation. She needed to get Julia out of the house. If she didn't, Sara might leave with her.

"You'll *try* to come by?" Julia asked. "I expected a little more than that."

"You don't understand," Sara said.

"I guess I don't," Julia said. "Why don't you explain it to me."

"It's Christmas. There are traditions."

"I hate to interrupt your little Norman Rockwell moment, darling, but are these traditions you actually want to participate in?" Julia asked.

"That isn't the point."

"What is the point?"

"Julia, don't do this to me. Don't make me choose between you or them. There's too much history there."

Julia paused. "I guess it is unfair. But I want to make love to you."

Sara cautioned her to keep her voice down, looking again at the door. As if on cue, Grady entered.

Sara pivoted toward the counter and gathered the dessert plates to take out to the dining room. Julia turned toward Grady.

"How have you been, Grady?"

Grady paused, looked at Julia, but didn't answer. "The kids are waiting for pie," Grady said to Sara. "Are you coming?"

"Well, I guess I'll be going," Julia said, walking toward the door. "Tell everyone I said goodbye and that I loved meeting them," she said to Sara. "And Grady, you haven't changed a bit," she added.

The look that passed between them had a story in it. A story that neither had bothered to tell Sara.

Julia left and Grady carried the stack of dessert plates and forks into the dining room. He said nothing to Sara before he left.

Sara stayed in the kitchen for a few seconds to pull herself together. She considered briefly jumping into the Volvo and following Julia. But Sara knew that if she ran away this time it would be for good.

Later that evening as Sara and Grady were getting ready for bed she experienced the full barrage of his silence. After Julia left he had been sullen for the rest of the evening even when the kids tried to joke him out of it.

"Well, that was unexpected," he said finally. "Julia just showing up out of the blue. Did you two plan this?"

"I had no idea she was coming," Sara said. *And if I had known of her plans, I would have talked her out of it,* was the part she didn't say.

"It's just like Julia to steal the show," he said.

"She wasn't trying to 'steal the show,'" Sara said. "She was just being herself."

"Right," Grady said sarcastically. He rolled over and turned off the light, as if Julia's visit was a lump of coal Santa had delivered in his Christmas stocking.

Sara lay in the dark processing the events of the last few hours. Julia was just a few blocks away. Sara traced the route in her mind. It would take her all of five minutes to get there. She could be in Julia's arms right now, instead of staring the bulk of Grady's back. She contemplated sneaking out. Grady wouldn't miss her. He was used to her middle of the night roamings by now.

Sara moved to the edge of the bed. Luke thumped his tail once as if to ask: *Is it time to get up already?* Sara stepped over him and quietly slipped on a pair of jeans and a sweater. She felt like a teenager sneaking out of the house to meet her beau. She grabbed her shoes and carried them through the dark house to the kitchen door. She took the Volvo keys from the hook and pushed on the door to unlatch it. It cracked loudly and Sara paused to see if Grady would appear with a baseball bat to fend off a potential burglar. Instead she heard only Luke's toenails on the wood floors. He arrived in the kitchen, wagging his tail in the pale spill-over of light from the streetlamp. He looked toward the closet where his leash was kept. Sara whispered for him to stay and he whimpered slightly.

A rush of cold air hit Sara from all directions. She had forgotten her coat and New England was already frigid by the end of December. But she didn't want to risk going back. She walked briskly to the Volvo and got inside. She was freezing. Her teeth began to chatter.

Where are those hot flashes when you need them? she thought.

She put the key in the ignition but something stopped her from starting the engine.

"I can't do this," she said out loud. The words penetrated the cold like smoke signals. Then she tasted a warm, salty tear as it touched her lips.

Chapter Twenty-Two

Julia opened the door at the Bed and Breakfast wearing her red kimono. "It's three o'clock. I expected you hours ago."

It was not the greeting Sara expected, but it was certainly, she quickly decided, the one she deserved. "Merry Christmas," Sara said as she walked past Julia and closed the door.

In Italy, Sara had followed Julia's lead but this was her territory. Julia stood facing Sara, her arms on her hips, cleavage exposed. She hated Julia at that moment for looking beautiful and radiant, even in her anger. This was going to be hard, but she had a mission to complete. Having Julia in Northampton made her realize how crazy their time in Italy had been. If called into a courtroom to explain that time, she would plead temporary insanity.

"What's going on with you?" Julia asked, her hands remaining on her hips.

"I'm glad you came," Sara said. "It helped me get clear on some things."

"I'm glad I came, too," Julia said. She lowered her arms and took a step closer. But Sara put her arm out like a   crossing guard. "Okay, it's obvious we're not going to get anywhere until you say what's on your mind," Julia said. "So tell me, what did it help you get clear on?"

"Us."

"Us?" Julia sat on the end of the bed.

For the first time Sara noticed her surroundings. A tastefully decorated Bed & Breakfast, Victorian furnishings. As straight-laced and rigid as Sara felt. "This is nice," she said.

"It's not Italy, but it will do." Julia patted the bed to invite Sara to sit, but Sara remained standing. She was tired. Exhausted, really. She had missed another night's sleep. Something she wasn't good at even as a college student pulling all-nighters before exams. Her body ached to recline, rest, release. To counter this need, Sara stood straighter, calling on her posture to bolster her courage.

"I have a gift for you," Julia said. She went over to her suitcase and pulled out a small wrapped present.

"Oh, I wish you hadn't done that," Sara said. "I didn't get you anything."

"It's okay. I just saw it in an antique shop in Florence and had to get it for you."

Sara's resolve weakened. She took the gift and unwrapped it slowly revealing a brown leather jewelry box. Sara hesitated before opening it. Inside, was a gold necklace of the Madonna and child.

"It's an heirloom piece," Julia said.

"It's exquisite," Sara said softly.

"It reminds me of the fountain and of you," Julia said.

Sara touched the raised image.

"Put it on," Julia said.

Sara let her take the necklace and fasten it around her neck.

"Do you like it?"

"I love it," Sara said. Then she forced herself to stand straighter. "But it doesn't change what I have to say," she added.

Julia returned to sit on the bed. "By the way, when did you start wearing a wig?" Julia asked. "I liked your real hair, the way it was in Italy."

Sara reached up and straightened the hair piece that hid the results of her latest round of chemo. With all the excitement of Julia coming she had forgotten the state of her health.

"It's a long story," Sara said. "One I can't go into right now."

Get on with it, the critical voice began in her head. *Do what you need to do*. At that moment Sara was grateful for the critical voice. But there was another part of her, a softer, more vulnerable part, that didn't have a voice. It was the part that was in love with Julia and the part that was willing to do anything to be with her.

"I think I know what you're getting ready to do," Julia said. "And I don't think it's a very good idea."

"It's for the best," Sara said. "It was just a crazy time. I enjoyed it. But I can't be with you anymore. That person in Italy wasn't really me."

"And this person is?" Julia asked. What happened to needing more time?"

Sara had to give Julia credit for staying calm. "There's nothing to discuss about this," Sara said. "I've made up my mind and I hope you can just accept it."

Her dialogue sounded like a scene from a bad movie, Sara being the actress delivering an unconvincing performance. Was this what she really wanted? Maybe not, but it was what had to be. There were too many consequences to loving Julia.

"Goodbye Julia. I hope we can still be friends." This sounded trite.

"What is going on with you?" Julia asked. "You're acting like you've been taken over by pod people or something."

"Don't be funny, Julia." *Or beautiful, for that matter*, she wanted to say. "This is hard enough."

"Sit down, Sweetie. Let's talk about this."

But Sara couldn't run the risk of sitting down. She might collapse in Julia's arms. Julia stood. Sara took a step closer to the door.

"I thought you loved me," Julia said.

"Of course I love you." Sara weakened. "But this isn't about love, Julia. I have responsibilities here."

At that moment, she couldn't remember exactly what these responsibilities were, but she clung to the idea of them just as she literally clutched the medallion of the virgin mother around her neck.

"So what you need doesn't matter, right?" Julia asked.

"Right," Sara said. "Since when do I get what I want?"

"When you decide that you deserve it," Julia said.

"Now isn't the time to be wise," Sara snapped.

"So what would you prefer? Do you want me to throw things? Yell obscenities." Julia sat back on the bed and crossed her legs.

"Maybe," Sara said. "I don't understand how you can be so calm."

"I trust that if we're meant to be together we will be."

Sara huffed her frustration. "I don't have the energy for this," she said. "Why can't you just be angry and unreasonable? Then it would be much easier to walk away. Instead, you're being all those things I love about you."

Julia smiled. "I love you, too."

Just leave, the voice began in her head. *Get out before you do something crazy again.* Sara placed her hand on the doorknob, but she couldn't turn it. Her feet were mired to the floor, stuck between staying and leaving. "I don't know what to do," Sara said softly.

"It's okay," Julia said. "We'll figure it out." She touched Sara's shoulder and kissed the back of her neck.

An exquisite, terrifying shudder ran down Sara's body. She turned toward Julia and surrendered to the moment.

The days were getting longer. Spring announced itself in bursts of pastel colors. The winter had proved longer and grayer than any Sara remembered. Her time with Julia at Christmas, four months before, now seemed imagined. Julia's emails had increased. Sara's had waned. Julia called Sara's cell phone leaving erotic messages that Sara savored and then quickly erased for fear that someone might hear them. Often Sara did not pick up when Julia called. She oscillated between the new and the old; between the unknown and the known. She was too old to change her life now, wasn't she?

Sara and Grady finished dinner and Sara stacked the dishes next to the sink. "I forgot to tell you, Doctor Morgan called while you were out walking Luke," Grady said. "He wants you to call him."

Sara's six-month check-up after the second round of chemo had been the day before. He had said he would phone her with the results. She found Doctor Morgan's business card in a stack of papers on the dining room table and sat on the steps in the hallway that separated the kitchen and dining room. She rarely took the stairs up to the second floor anymore, since only the kids bedrooms were up there. But now Grady was talking about renovating the rooms. Knocking down walls and creating a den. It would be their biggest project yet. In Sara's view, this was a clear sign that they were in trouble.

Sara traced the edges of Doctor Morgan's card. Why had she been so intent about going through this alone? She wished now that she had told Julia. That's what people who loved each other did, wasn't it? Shared the good and the bad?

Sara picked up the cordless phone to dial the number. Regardless of the results, something had to change. A year before she had come to a crossroads. She couldn't afford to turn back this time. If the cancer didn't kill her, her indecision would.

"What are you doing?" Grady asked as he walked around the corner. He had his measuring tape to go upstairs.

She put down the phone and slid the business card into her pocket. The time had come to be honest.

"I know I've been distant lately," she said to Grady.

"Distant?" Grady asked.

"Since Italy," Sara said.

Her trip had been months before. Some of the longest months of her life, except for the two days at Christmas that Julia was there. Sara gazed at the throw rug at the foot of the stairs, as if her words were scattered on the floor in Scrabble pieces that she had to arrange before they counted for anything.

Stillness pervaded the background of their lives. Grady's impatience was visible. He jiggled his keys. What she was about to say had nothing and everything to do with her latest doctor visit and the test results she was about to receive.

"Grady, something happened in Italy last summer." Her confession, rehearsed for months, now sounded contrived, like a line in a badly written romance novel.

"What happened?" he said. His voice sounded cautious.

Sara hesitated. Was it too late to close the door she had just opened? Yet something inside her made her keep going. "I found something in Italy I don't think I can give up." Her voice quivered. She wanted it to sound stronger.

Grady's caution changed into irritation. His eyes narrowed. "And you're just now realizing this?"

Sara was walking dangerously close to the edge of a cliff. She wanted to jump. At the same time, she wanted someone to pull her back to safety.

"Grady, this is going to sound crazy . . . but I think I found my life there."

His frown deepened. "You're always speaking in riddles, Sara. Just give it to me in English."

Her introspection lacked the practicality Grady valued most. But she didn't back down. "In Italy I was a totally different person," she said.

"What are you trying to tell me?" he asked, his patience now ragged, like a pair of old jeans where skin shows through the knees.

"I fell in love," she said, surprised by her deeper confession.

"You fell in love?" His eyes locked onto hers. It was both strange and uncomfortable to have his undivided attention. He studied Sara like a tool he was unsure how to operate. "I suppose Julia introduced you to him," he said finally.

It angered Sara that he thought she would never have the courage to do this on her own. "Yes, in a way, I guess she did," Sara said.

Grady jiggled his keys again.

"Would you please stop that?"

The jiggling ceased.

"I think the someone I met was me," Sara said boldly.

"Where do you come up with this psychological bullshit?" His voice was low, like the growl of a dog sensing an intruder.

It occurred to Sara how refreshing it was to finally see an honest emotion coming from him. "This has been coming for years," she said. "You know it has. This didn't just happen because I went away to Italy."

"You sound ridiculous." His anger darted toward her.

But her chest felt lighter, as if the truth was liberating her. "We had to face our marriage sooner or later," she said. "Italy just accelerated things."

"So what happened in Italy?" he asked again.

Too late to turn back, she plunged forward with the truth. "I fell in love with Julia."

He smiled at first, as if she were joking. But then his expression changed and silence pervaded the room like a poison gas released to render them helpless.

"I didn't want to lie about it anymore," Sara said softly. "I felt I owed you more than that."

He smiled a half-smile, as though struck by something ironic. "I don't know what to say."

"Maybe you could just say what you feel."

He laughed a short laugh and walked into the dining room and opened the bottom door of the china cabinet where they had kept an assortment of liquor over the years. He took out a bottle of Irish whiskey and went into the kitchen to pour himself a drink. When he came back into the hallway he swallowed the drink dramatically like an actor playing the part of a jilted lover in an old Hollywood movie.

"You want me to say what I feel?" His tone rose. "Well, how about this, Sara. I feel screwed. After twenty-five years of marriage, you're in love with someone else? And that someone else is Julia? Since when are you gay, Sara?"

The distaste in his question was pungent. Sara stared down his judgment. "That's not what this is about," she said.

"The hell it isn't!" He finished his drink. "Is that why she visited at Christmas? So you two could have a little fling?"

Sara lowered her eyes. Being with Julia at Christmas had only confused her more. In Italy, her betrayal of Grady and her life in the States had seemed less of an issue. After all, hadn't Grady done the same? Except he had had an affair in the same town and with someone in his office, right under her nose.

Sara followed Grady into the kitchen. He sat at the kitchen table, his head in his hands. Sara thought of Max and Melanie's table at the farmhouse. That last morning in Siena she had awoken early and gone downstairs and carved her name in the wood right next to Julia's. Over the last seven months she had thought of it often, the coarse letters of her name beside Julia's, a tactile memory of their closeness.

"I'm not good at things like this," he said. "I never know what to say." He lifted his head and stared at his hands, as if looking at Sara held too big of a challenge.

"I'd really like it if we could just be honest with one another," Sara said.

"Honesty isn't everything it's cracked up to be," he said. His sarcasm ended in a brief laugh.

"Maybe not," she said. "But I think we should try."

"It's just so unexpected, Sara. What are we supposed to do now?"

"I'm not sure," she said truthfully.

The thought entered her mind that this was the first real conversation they had had in years. In the past they had traded sentences with each other and now there were paragraphs.

"So you go to Italy for a couple of weeks and our marriage is over?" he asked. He didn't sound particularly disappointed.

"This was happening way before Italy," she said again. "And way before I got cancer."

"Yeah, the cancer thing," he said. "What did Doctor Morgan say?"

"I haven't called him back yet." The truth was, she didn't want what Doctor Morgan said to keep her from doing what she needed to do. "The cancer diagnosis helped me see things more clearly," she continued. "I couldn't fool myself anymore about what was working and what wasn't. Life is too short to tread water because you're afraid of what's onshore."

He looked unimpressed with her armchair analysis of the situation. "Maybe we should talk this over with that therapist we're paying thousands of dollars a year," he said.

"Maybe we should," she said.

Grady frowned. "I hate shrinks," he said under his breath. "It doesn't seem to have done us much good."

"Actually, I think it's too late for counseling, Grady. You need things I can't give you anymore. And you deserve more than someone just going through the motions."

Grady lowered his eyes. "Is this because of what happened with Marcia?"

"It has nothing to do with that," Sara said. "But even then we should have known something was wrong."

Marcia Hammond, Sara thought.

Until now, Sara had not known it was her. But Sara had met her once at one of Grady's terminally boring insurance conventions in Atlantic City. It suddenly occurred to her how much Marcia Hammond resembled Julia. A shorter, less beautiful version, but still there were similarities. Could it be possible that for all these years he had been dealing with Julia's ghost?

"What happened between you and Julia?" Sara asked.

He shrugged and brushed a hand through his hair.

"That day she left, she said something weird happened between you two, but she didn't tell me the details," Sara said. "And when she showed up at Christmas you were practically morose."

"You two didn't talk about this in Italy?" His lips tightened. "Or maybe you were busy with other things." He chucked a humorless laugh.

"What happened?" she asked again, not willing to shift the focus back on her. Not until she got the truth.

He hesitated and looked out the window, but then after a few seconds he started to talk. "She was in her bedroom putting stuff in boxes, getting ready to move. She was more interested in her packing than me, but that was nothing new. I think I told her she couldn't just leave like this and she said something like she didn't have a choice; that her dad got a teaching job that he couldn't turn down."

Grady pushed back the kitchen chair and turned to face Sara. "Then I told her that maybe she could stay with you until she finished Beacon High. Anything, you know, to keep her around. But she just said that things change, and that I should just get used to it. But I didn't want things to change. I'd been in love with her since I was thirteen."

He glanced at Sara to see her reaction. But she had no reaction. Except to be struck by how clear the memory was for him, as if it had just happened.

He continued. "I got it in my head that I had to prove to her how much I loved her. So I kissed her, but she pushed me away. Like an idiot I tried to kiss her again. I think I even backed her up against the wall. I know it was totally stupid, but I just kept trying to prove to her how much I loved her and how much she needed to stay. I kept at it until she yelled at me about how I'd gone nuts. And about how she never wanted to see me again. Then I got desperate and told her how I'd been saving up money for an apartment for us to live in some day. And that totally flipped her out. She started screaming at me to get out. And I did. I left. And I never saw her again. That is, until Christmas."

Sara reached over to touch Grady's hand but he moved it away. "That must have been very hard for you," Sara said. It was hard to imagine Grady that passionate, that out of control.

"Then after that, you and me went out on the 4th of July and ended up behind Beacon making out in the back seat of my Chevy," Grady began again. "When we started hanging out together, it was almost like having Julia there, because you two had been practically joined at the hip, you know? Over the years I just got comfortable with you. I never got around to dating anybody else. Maybe we wouldn't have gotten married if I had. But we made the best of things, didn't we? That's what's important. We made the best of things."

With this admission, the tension cleared from the room.

"I think we're a lot alike," Sara said finally. "I've been making the best of things, too. And you know what's also sad? I think this is the most we've ever shared with each other our whole married life. We've never really shared anything that's going on below the surface, you know?"

Grady nodded. A lot of things made sense to Sara now. How devastated Grady had been after Julia left and how, at first, he had constantly asked if she had heard from her. Several weeks after that they had begun to date. A couple of years after that they were married. He had wanted Sara to send Julia an invitation to the wedding, but she had refused. Julia was in England. She had a new life. Perhaps Sara had felt jilted, too.

Silence followed. The scene, although sad, felt complete. Grady and Sara sat across from each other while the clock in the kitchen ticked down the remaining seconds of their marriage.

"To tell you the truth," Grady said finally, "I always thought one of us would end up with Julia. I just hoped it would be me."

Chapter Twenty-Three

The Tuscan countryside was alive with sunflowers as Sara drove the silver rental car toward Max and Melanie's farmhouse. Julia's last email had said that she was visiting Max and Melanie for an extended stay. She had brought her paints and Max had set her up a studio in one of the guest rooms overlooking the courtyard.

Sara had gone to Florence first, but Francesca had told her that Julia was still in the country. So Sara bought a map, circled her destination in yellow highlighter, and had found her way there. As she drove up the driveway she remembered that frantic night she had contemplated ramming herself into the olive trees because of the revelation of her love for Julia. She had come a long way since then. She was in remission again, a pronouncement Sara had taken as getting a second chance in life, and she had every intention of honoring whatever time she had left.

There were no cars in the driveway and Sara wondered briefly if she had come all this way for nothing. Julia was making more trips to London and Rome to sell her paintings. Maybe she had missed her. Sara knocked at the front door and waited, but no one answered. She thought she would check the courtyard just in case. When she walked through the gate, she saw Julia standing with her back to her. She stood in front of a large canvas etching in the outline of the fountain.

"What are you two doing back so soon?" Julia called over her shoulder, assuming that Max and Melanie had returned.

"Well actually it's been close to a year, so it doesn't quite feel like soon enough," Sara said.

Julia turned to face her, brush still in hand. "Oh, my God!" The shock on Julia's face turned to joy. She quickly put down the brush and palette and came to greet Sara.

"I know you're not too keen on surprises, but I love them!" Julia smiled.

Sara rested the large shopping bag next to her that she had carried all the way from New England. She opened her arms. They embraced and kissed. When they parted, the joy of seeing Sara was still on Julia's face.

"What are you doing here?" she asked.

"It seemed like the right thing to do," Sara said.

Julia laughed. "Look at you!" she said.

"A new life requires a new look," Sara smiled.

A physical transformation had accompanied Sara's decision to return to Italy. Sara wore a red linen dress accentuating her cleavage and her reconstructed breast, an adopted twin sister to the other. Long earrings dangled just above her shoulders. She had burned her wig in the fireplace in New England. Her natural hair was longer and blonder with a few gray hairs mixed in. Not to mention the medallion Julia gave her that she never took off.

"I went to Florence and you weren't there," Sara said. "So I went to Francesca's shop and she told me where you were. She sends her love, by the way, and wanted me to tell you that Roberto and Bella are fine."

Julia had not stopped smiling. "How long can you stay?"

Sara shrugged. "How long do you want me to stay?"

"Don't kid around with me, Sweetie."

"Well it seems I've run away from home. And this time it may be for good." Sara smiled. "I left Grady," she began again. "Or I should say it was a mutual decision. He wasn't happy either, it turns out. And I quit my job and cashed in my retirement from the school system to come here. I also told my children about us. They were in shock at first. But they're getting used to it. I think it made it easier since they got to meet you at Christmas. And, of course, everyone wants to visit. Anyway, I'm hoping you still want to explore where this might take us."

Julia laughed a hearty laugh. "Definitely," she said. Julia glanced at the large shopping bag next to Sara's feet. "That must have been hell getting on the plane."

Sara reached into the bag and took out a large globe like the one from their childhood that had sparked many adventures in their imaginations. But Sara was ready for the real thing now. "I hope you're up for an adventure," Sara said.

Julia smiled. They embraced again, the lady in stone witnessing the embrace. Sara had missed her, too. In the background of their reunion, the fountain offered her consent.

Thank you for reading!

Dear Reader,

I hope you enjoyed *Seeking Sara Summers*. This novel was the first one I wrote for adults, and I continue to hear from readers who let me know how Sara and Julia's story resonated with them.

As an author, I love to hear from readers. To me, as the story travels from writer to reader and then back again, it is like completing a circle. You are the reason I write. So feel free to tell me what you liked about Sara and Julia's story, what you loved, even what you wish I'd done differently.

You can write me at susan@susangabriel.com or message me on my Facebook author page: www.facebook.com/SusanGabrielAuthor.

Finally, I have a favor to ask. Please consider leaving a review of *Seeking Sara Summers* on Amazon, Goodreads, Nook, Google Books, iTunes, Kobo or elsewhere. Reviews help other readers take a chance on a book or an author they may not be familiar with. A review doesn't have to be long or "literary." Just two or three heartfelt sentences is enough.

Thanks so much for reading *Seeking Sara Summers* and for spending time with me.

In gratitude,
Susan Gabriel

P.S. Do you want to get notified when I publish new books? I would be happy to email you when new books become available (two or three times a year at most). Please sign up here today: https://www.susangabriel.com/new-books/

Questions from Readers

Answered by author Susan Gabriel

Is anything in *Seeking Sara Summers* based on real life experiences or is the story purely all imagination?

As writers, our work can't help but be autobiographical, simply in terms of what we notice in the world. I notice sounds and smells and see things in ways that are totally unique to me. My imagination is the instrument I use to tell a story, so it is always a reflection of me in some way. Length of paragraph, turn of phrase, word choice, the metaphors I choose, are all my tiny fingerprint.

That said, *Seeking Sara Summers* is about a woman who finds herself in a marriage that isn't fulfilling and then who falls in love with her best friend. This happened to me, yet I fictionalized the story, otherwise it would be way too boring.

At the first writer's conference I attended, a presenter encouraged aspiring writers to create the book we wished we'd had available while going through a difficult time in our lives. *Seeking Sara Summers* is the book I wish I had found in the library or bookstores at that time. I needed a road map, and I didn't have one. So twenty years later I created for readers a roadmap wrapped inside what I hope is a compelling story.

Can you comment on the significance of the statues of the Virgin Mary that appear throughout *Seeking Sara Summers*?

Italy is a very Catholic and patriarchal country, although not that many people still attend church—at least that's what a well-dressed Italian woman told me a few years ago on a train to Milan. But statues of Mary are everywhere. To me, her image in the book is a representation of the divine feminine, a kind of patron saint for women. Since this story is ultimately about two women who choose love over cultural rules or taboos, it made sense for her to be there and watch over them and perhaps even wish them well.

What genre do you feel most at ease writing in, if any?

Over the years, I have written in several different genres including children's fiction, adult fiction, short stories, plays and poetry. As far as categories, you can find me in literary fiction, southern fiction and coming-of-age stories. Right now I am claiming my roots and writing mostly southern fiction. I like to write about families and strong women in settings I have lived in. So at this point my stories take place on the coastal regions of South Carolina (I lived in Charleston for 14 years), in the mountains of Tennessee (where I grew up) or the mountains of western North Carolina (where I live today).

How do you like to approach your writing when starting a new project? Do you do outlines, and breakdown scenes, or do you just leap straight into writing the narrative?

Most of my stories begin with a voice. If I am lucky, I will hear a character's voice and luckier still if they begin to tell me their story. I am an intuitive writer and have a rich imagination, so it usually begins with a dialogue or a first-person voice. I don't do outlines. Creating a story is a total leap into my imagination.

The characters develop as I get to know them. Over time I learn their family history, their personal habits and their motivation. However, I rarely know where a story is going after I start it. Nor do I know how it will end up. A first draft is like getting the bones in, like a skeleton, and then subsequent drafts are spent putting flesh on the bones.

Sometimes, I even dream about the characters of whatever book I am working on. While writing *Seeking Sara Summers*, Grady walked by in a dream and waved to me. I thought this was very generous of him since he isn't the most sympathetic of characters in the book.

What did you do before you became a writer?

I started out as a professional musician and then became a teacher for at-risk kids, before getting a graduate degree in counseling. I was a licensed psychotherapist in private practice for ten years. I did good work, but one day I realized that if I didn't follow what was deep in my heart and pursue writing, I would die with regrets.

When I began to write, I started out writing children's books (ages 10 and up). I think I started with juvenile fiction because writing a novel for adults seemed much more daunting. But that was a good process for me in those early years because I learned to put together a story with a beginning, middle and an end. I also learned what engages readers of all ages: a really good story.

What was the most fun part about writing *Seeking Sara Summers*?

I traveled to Italy to do research for the book in 2004, and then the book came out in 2008. It was an amazing trip and many of the places I experienced ended up in the book.

What's your favorite thing about being a writer?

The writing process (as opposed to things like rewriting and marketing). I love it when a cast of characters show up, and I get to tell their story. I love that period of time when I am totally in my imagination, seeing the story play out in front of me while I write it down. I lose track of time and look up and it's suddenly three hours later.

Also, I love hearing from readers who tell me they couldn't put down one of my books and got swept up into the world of the story and were moved by it. This is a very special moment. I think stories have the power to heal and inspire. And if I accomplish even a tiny bit of that, then I have done my job.

* * *

Susan loves to hear from readers! If you would reach her with a comment or question, you can contact her here:
 https://www.susangabriel.com/contact-author/

Other books by Susan Gabriel

The Secret Sense of Wildflower

A novel

"A quietly powerful story, at times harrowing, but ultimately a joy to read." - Kirkus Reviews, starred review (for books of remarkable merit)

Named to Kirkus Reviews' Best Books of 2012.

Set in 1940s Appalachia, *The Secret Sense of Wildflower* tells the story of Louisa May "Wildflower" McAllister whose life has been shaped around the recent death of her beloved father in a sawmill accident. While her mother hardens in her grief, Wildflower and her three sisters must cope with their loss themselves, as well as with the demands of daily survival. Despite these hardships, Wildflower has a resilience that is forged with humor, a love of the land, and an endless supply of questions to God. When Johnny Monroe, the town's teenage ne'er-do-well, sets his sights on Wildflower, she must draw on the strength of her relations, both living and dead, to deal with his threat.

With prose as lush and colorful as the American South, *The Secret Sense of Wildflower* is a powerful and poignant southern novel, brimming with energy and angst, humor and hope.

Praise for *The Secret Sense of Wildflower*

"Louisa May immerses us in her world with astute observations and wonderfully turned phrases, with nary a cliché to be found. She could be an adolescent Scout Finch, had Scout's father died unexpectedly and her life taken a bad turn...By necessity, Louisa May grows up quickly, but by her secret sense, she also understands forgiveness. A quietly powerful story, at times harrowing but ultimately a joy to read."
– Kirkus Reviews

"A soulful narrative to keep the reader emotionally charged and invested. *The Secret Sense of Wildflower* is eloquent and moving tale chock-filled with themes of inner strength, family and love."
– Maya Fleischmann, indiereader.com

"I've never read a story as dramatically understated that sings so powerfully and honestly about the sense of life that stands in tribute to bravery as Susan Gabriel's, *The Secret Sense of Wildflower*...When fiction sings, we must applaud."
– T. T. Thomas, author of *A Delicate Refusal*

"The story is powerful, very powerful. Excellent visuals, good drama. I raced to get to the conclusion...but didn't really want to read the last few pages because then it would be over! I look forward to Gabriel's next offering."
– Nancy Purcell, Author

"Just finished this with tears streaming down my face. Beautifully written with memorable characters who show resilience in the face of tragedy. I couldn't put this down and will seek Susan Gabriel's other works. This is truly one of the best books I've read in a very long time." – A.C.

"An interesting story enhanced by great writing, this book was a page turner. It captures life in the Tennessee mountains truthfully but not harshly. I would recommend this book to anyone who enjoys historical fiction." – E. Jones

"I don't even know how to tell you what I love about this book --- the incredible narrator? The heartbreaking and inspiring storyline? The messages about hope, wisdom, family and strength? All of those!! Everything about it!" – K. Peck

"Lovely, soul stirring novel. I absolutely could not put it down! Beautifully descriptive, evocative story told in the voice of Wildflower, a young girl of the mountains, set in a wild yet beautiful 1940's mountain town, holds you captive from the start. I had to wait to write my review, as I was crying too hard to see!" – V.C.

"I write novels, too, but this writer is fantastic. The story is authentic and gripping. Her voice through the child, Wildflower, is captivating. This story would make a great movie. I love stories that portray life changing tragedy and pain coupled with power of the human spirit to survive and continue to love and forgive. Bravo! Susan. Please write more and more." –Judi D.

"This is a wonderful story that will make you laugh, cry, and cheer." –T.B. Markinson

"I was pretty blown away by how good this book is. I didn't read it with any expectations, hadn't heard anything about it really, so when I read it, I realized from page one that it is a well written, powerful book." – Quixotic Magpie

"If you liked *Little Women* or if you love historical fiction and coming-of-age novels, this is the book for you. Definitely add *The Secret Sense of Wildflower* to your TBR pile; you won't regret it."
– PandaReads

"Bottom line: A great story about a strong character!"
– Meg, A Bookish Affair

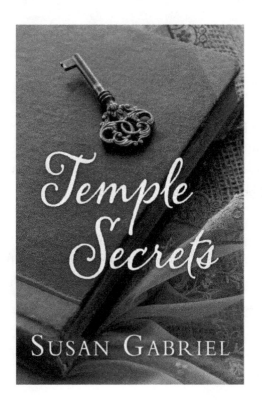

Temple Secrets
A novel

Fans of *The Help* and *Midnight in the Garden of Good and Evil* will delight in this comic novel of family secrets by acclaimed writer, Susan Gabriel.

Every family has secrets, but the elite Temple family of Savannah has more than most. To maintain their influence, they've also been documenting the indiscretions of other prestigious southern families, dating as far back as the Civil War. When someone begins leaking these tantalizing tidbits to the newspaper, the entire city of Savannah, Georgia is rocking with secrets.

The current keeper of the secrets and matriarch of the Temple clan is Iris, a woman of unpredictable gastrointestinal illnesses and an extra streak of meanness that even the ghosts in the Temple mansion avoid. When Iris unexpectedly dies, the consequences are far flung and significant, not only to her family—who get in line to inherit the historic family mansion—but to Savannah itself.

At the heart of the story is Old Sally, an expert in Gullah folk magic, who some suspect cast a voodoo curse on Iris. At 100 years of age, Old Sally keeps a wise eye over the whole boisterous business of secrets and the settling of Iris's estate.

In the Temple family, nothing is as it seems, and everyone has a secret.

Available in paperback, ebook and audiobook.

Praise for *Temple Secrets*

"*Temple Secrets* is a page-turner of a story that goes deeper than most on the subjects of equality, courage and dignity. There were five or six characters to love and a few to loathe. Gabriel draws Queenie, Violet, Spud and Rose precisely, with a narrative dexterity that is amazingly and perfectly sparse while achieving an impact of fullness and depth. Their interactions with the outside world and one another are priceless moments of hilarious asides, well-aimed snipes and a plethora of sarcasms.

"What happens when the inevitable inequities come about amongst the Haves, the Have Nots and the Damn-Right-I-Will-Have? When some people have far too much time, wealth and power and not enough humanness and courage? Oh, the answers

Gabriel provides are as delicious as Violet's peach turnovers, and twice as addicting! I highly recommend this novel."

– T.T. Thomas

"Susan Gabriel shines once again in this fascinating tale of a family's struggle to break free from their past. Filled with secrets, betrayals, and tragedy, the author weaves an intricate storyline that will keep you hooked." - R. Krug

"I loved this book! I literally couldn't put it down. The characters are fabulous and the story line has plenty of twists and turns making it a great read. I was born and raised in the south so I have an affinity for stories that are steeped in the southern culture. *Temple Secrets* nails it. All I needed was a glass of sweet tea to go with it." – Carol Clay

"The setting is rich and sensuous, and the secrets kept me reading with avid interest until most of them were revealed. I read the book in just a few days because I really didn't want to put it down. It is filled with characters who are funny, tragic, unpredictable and nuanced, and I must admit that I really came to know and love some of them by the end of the story." – Nancy Richards

"I was glued from the first moment that I began reading. The book accurately portrays many of the attitudes of the Old South including the intricate secrets and "skeletons in the closet" that people often wish to deny. Each character is fascinating and I loved watching each one evolve as the story unfolded. This was one of those books that I did not want to finish as it was so much fun to be involved in the action."

– Lisa Patty

"I just finished reading *Temple Secrets* today and I truly hated for it to end! Susan Gabriel writes with such warmth and humor, and this book is certainly no exception. I loved getting to know the characters and the story was full of humor and suspense."

– Carolyn Tenn

About the Author

Susan Gabriel is an acclaimed writer who lives in the mountains of North Carolina. Her novel, *The Secret Sense of Wildflower*, earned a starred review ("for books of remarkable merit") from Kirkus Reviews and was also named to their list of Best Books of 2012.

She is also the author of *Temple Secrets*, *Lily's Song* and other novels. Discover more about Susan at susangabriel.com

Also by Susan Gabriel

Fiction

The Secret Sense of Wildflower
(a Kirkus Reviews Best Book of 2012)

Lily's Song
(sequel to *The Secret Sense of Wildflower*)

Temple Secrets

Trueluck Summer

Grace, Grits and Ghosts: Southern Short Stories

Quentin & the Cave Boy

Circle of the Ancestors

Nonfiction

Fearless Writing for Women

Available at all booksellers
in print, ebook and audio formats.

CPSIA information can be obtained
at www.ICGtesting.com
Printed in the USA
BVHW091732281022
650371BV00006BA/416

9 780615 222073